REVENGE
FROM
BEYOND

Dennis Wong

The Author of **REVENGE FROM BEYOND** freely acknowledges his debt to the late Robert Van Gulik, the author of many detective novels with a Chinese background. Dennis Wong's book, however, stands on its own, supported by a strong plot and good characterization.

Struggling against his own inexperience as a judge, the protagonist, Judge Quan, succeeds in solving a very difficult case, involving an attractive (and hostile) widow and the son of the Chinese Emperor's principal adviser. The judge's work is made particularly difficult by the prejudices of the local population.

DENNIS WONG was born in Singapore and his family migrated to Australia in 1977. He holds a degree in Applied Mathematics and Computer Science, and has worked in Information Technology for the past twenty years. He lives in Sydney, Australia with his wife and son.

A yearning to find answers to life's basic questions led to Wong's interest in spirituality as early as High School. In University, this grew into a passion for Buddhism and subsequently an interest in Chinese culture, myths and beliefs.

In 1985, a Chinese Crime Novel by Robert Van Gulik captured Dennis Wong's imagination. Many years later, he completed his own first novel in the same genre, **Revenge From Beyond**, which he entered for the Proverse Prize in 2010. He is now working on a second novel, also set against the backdrop of the Chinese Han Empire.

Wong's writing embodies his interest in life. A person, with high moral ideals, starts his Magistrate's career as an under-dog. He confronts numerous obstacles and gradually resolves them by deductive thought and spiritual principles.

Proverse Prize Semi-Finalist 2010

REVENGE FROM BEYOND

Proverse Prize Semi-Finalist 2010

Dennis Wong

ORIGINAL ILLUSTRATIONS BY DENNIS WONG

Proverse Hong Kong

Revenge from Beyond
by Dennis Wong
2nd pbk ed., published in Hong Kong by Proverse Hong Kong, Feb. 2016.
Copyright © Proverse Hong Kong, February 2016.
ISBN: 978-988-8228-26-3
Printed by CreateSpace.

1st pub. in pbk in Hong Kong by Proverse Hong Kong, November 2011.
Copyright © Proverse Hong Kong, November 2011.
ISBN 978-988-19932-5-0

1st edition distribution (Hong Kong and worldwide):
The Chinese University Press of Hong Kong,
The Chinese University of Hong Kong, Shatin, NT, Hong Kong SAR.
E-mail: cup-bus@cuhk.edu.hk; Web site: www.chineseupress.com
Distribution (United Kingdom): Christine Penney, Stratford-upon-Avon,
Warwickshire CV37 6DN, England. Email: <chrisp@proversepublishing.com>

Enquiries: Proverse Hong Kong, P. O. Box 259, Tung Chung Post Office,
Tung Chung, Lantau Island, NT, Hong Kong SAR, China.
E-mail: proverse@netvigator.com; Web site: www.proversepublishing.com

The right of Dennis Wong to be identified as the author of this work has been
asserted by him in accordance with
the Copyright, Designs and Patents Act 1988.
The right of H.H. Judge Garry Tallentire to be identified as the author of
"Preface" has been asserted by him in accordance with
the Copyright, Designs and Patents Act 1988.

Illustrations including cover illustrations by the Author, Dennis Wong.
Page design by Proverse Hong Kong.
Picture pages design by Artist Hong Kong Company.
Cover design, Proverse Hong Kong and Artist Hong Kong Company.

British Library Cataloguing in Publication Data.
A catalopgue record for this book is available from the British Library.

Revenge from Beyond

CONTENTS

TABLE OF ILLUSTRATIONS

CHARACTERS

Beggar
Candidate Soong: Son of Soong Fu-liu. A Candidate for the
Judiciary Examination.
Chu Fan-shing: A murdered artist.
Chu Hong-li: Widow of Chu Fan-shing
Chen Tsu-wee: Coroner and Sergeant to Judge Quan.
E-Lung: Constable to Judge Quan.
Examiner Shao: Local district Judiciary Examination Marker.
Hermit
Hotel Guild-Master / Sheng Lu-ching
Judge Quan / Quan Wu-meng. Magistrate of Sui-chou district.
Rice-merchant He
Siu Lu-ming: a farmer's widow.
Soong Fu-liu / Elder Soong. Principal adviser to the Emperor.
Warden Xu. Warden of the North-Western sector of Sui-chou.
Yan Li-shing: A thief who stole from his neighbour.

PREFACE

"Revenge From Beyond" is a wonderful insight into the role of the Judge/Magistrate in Imperial China. Set in the Tang Dynasty, it portrays a judicial system of some sophistication yet steeped in brutality and unchallengeable power. As a member of a modern Western Judiciary I was fascinated by both the differences from and the similarites to our system. The differences are perhaps more self evident and startling – the absolute unassailable authority wielded by Judge Quan over his court/tribunal, the arbitrary, and by our standards, barbaric punishments inflicted on those who offended him or the law, the methodology of arriving at a verdict and the manner in which he was able and, indeed, required to both investigate and judge. Perhaps the strangest of all was that, for serious cases, the sentence was handed down, not by the Judge but by the Provincial Prefect! The similarities are very surprising – the use of forensic evidence provided by the coroner, the formality of the proceedings, and the use and reliance on self confessions. There is, of course, no concept of Independence of the Judiciary. The Judge was very much the local embodiment of the Divine Emperor!

The characters in this book are strong, interesting and convincing. Judge Quan is a very human character – learned, dedicated and so very conscious of the responsibilities of his high office. At times his near absolute power seems to cause him unease, craving public support and understanding. He is supported in his endeavours by his loyal aides, the clever Coroner and the brave constable. Together they are a formidable team of crime fighters. Added to this we have almost classical villains, driven by money, lust, or both. Then comes the whole populace of the town, from which the author draws some very interesting supporting characters.

The plot itself, whilst somewhat predictable from an early stage, in its general application, if not in detail, is an absolute delight! Skillfully the author peels away the layers, introducing elements of mysticism, and arrives at the denouncing of the perpetrators! This in turn leads to their harrowing and bloody fate. Some may find this to be entirely deserved.

All in all this is a well-crafted satisfying read that both entertains and provides a vivd insight into the Judicial system of

China in the Tang Dynasty. It is my profound hope that this is not the last we will hear of Judge Quan and I look forward to further adventures.

H.H. Judge Garry Tallentire,
The District Court,
Hong Kong.

AUTHOR'S INTRODUCTION

Many books have been written about the work of Chinese Judges and the Judiciary systems of past Chinese Dynasties. Many of these books, however, have been written in Chinese. Very few have been written in English, although Dr Fu Manchu and Judge Dee do come to mind.

What follows is a Chinese crime story that I hope will be of interest to the Western public. First, it describes the life, long hours and dedication of a Judiciary Judge, whose main responsibilities were to uphold law and order and collect taxes. He also had a multitude of other tasks such as healthcare, maintaining accurate records of births and deaths, and the collection of taxes. In the Western sense, the Judge was Governor of the whole town.

Second, the book's portrayal of Eastern customs and beliefs provides insights into the common thinking of the Chinese people and access to ideas that have been fostered and nurtured over many Dynasties.

Third, Chinese stories invariably include matters of a mystical nature, including ghosts, premonitions and superstitions. *Revenge from Beyond* is no exception. For many years, in my experience, talk of ghosts and beings from other planets as having real existence seemed to be taboo in sensible society. But with the success of Western TV programmes such as *The X-Files*, I find that these subjects, previously taboo, are widely addressed in films, books and magazines.

But there are also negative elements. Many Chinese stories are very long, some in excess of ten volumes, including innumerable personalities. The present author has excluded such elements on the grounds that they might confuse the reader.

I hope that *Revenge from Beyond* will bring to the Western public aspects of ancient Chinese society in a way that is new and fresh. I hope this book will be the first in a series of books describing the career of Judge Quan.

Judge Quan is a fictitious figure, although some events in this book are based on actual crimes committed in ancient times. A bibliography at the conclusion of the novel reveals my sources. I have also referred to certain Chinese beliefs and superstitions.

9

The naming convention for a Chinese person is such that the surname comes first, followed by the person's first given name and the Western concept of the middle name. So Quan Wu-meng indicates that the person's surname is Quan and his given name is Wu-meng.

The author's aim is to mirror many aspects of Chinese life in ancient times. By today's standards, some of these may seem crude and "politically incorrect". They include females not being treated equally and the use of harsh language, tortures and punishments. I have kept these, so as to reflect, as accurately as possible, the lives and systems of a bygone era. To exclude such aspects would be to steal from the reader an opportunity to understand, a little more, the lives of people in that era.

Revenge from Beyond brings Eastern lives to Western people. I hope that many readers will enjoy the book as much as I enjoyed writing it.

Dennis H. F. Wong

CHAPTER ONE

Be wise; be diligent; for the Empire is vast and grand.
Value those who are your friends;
be vigilant against those who are not.

As the green luminous mist slowly crawled its way towards the Judge, a sense of imminent death seemed to hover over the bridge.

Slowly, the mist began to move and the Judge was able to make out what appeared to be a female body, gradually emerging out of the gloom.

Suddenly, without a moment's notice, the mist took on a fully-formed female shape. A cool breeze blew a few strands of long white hair across her luminous face. Her loose white gown blew freely in the air, as she motioned the Judge to come towards her with long and slender fingers.

As if hypnotized by her mysterious beauty, he stepped forward. But the bridge swayed suddenly, shifted by a sudden gust of wind. The Judge struggled to maintain his balance as he heard the noise of planks breaking apart. He looked down and realized to his horror that the bridge was collapsing beneath him. Unable to maintain his balance any longer, he fell headlong into the dark abyss below, casting a despairing look at the female shape. Her face was no longer lovely. In its place he saw a skull. It squealed with laughter at the hapless, falling Judge.

He heard himself scream as he awoke behind his library desk. Cold sweat flowed freely from the Judge's forehead as he struggled to his feet and stomped clumsily towards the window opposite. Sliding it open, he felt a cool gentle breeze from outside the library. As he looked below the paper-covered lattice window, he saw to his satisfaction that the tea-stove was still well alight. He poured himself a cup of tea and drank it in one quick swallow. The cool breeze and the aromatic smell of the tea worked gradually to clear the Judge's head as he slowly made his way back to his desk.

In the cool ambience of the room, he reflected that the dream was indeed a fearful one. Was there any significance in it? Perhaps it was a warning to him to maintain his composure and concentration in this, his first posting; to Sui-chou, a remote south-western district of the Tang Empire, where the law might be lax and the people restless.

The only son of a poor farmer, Quan Wu-Meng had been an industrious boy. Although audacious and strong-willed, he had been unable to prevent the senseless murder of his parents at the hands of a corrupt local official. Torn by grief, he was adopted by his Uncle, a herbalist, who raised him as his own son and guided him through the arduous judiciary education system.

Having passed his District Selection Examination at the young age of eighteen, Quan made the long journey to the Prefecture and sat for three days in solitude in a small hot cell to complete his Provincial Examination. Having passed this examination and been given the title of "The Exalted Man", he was then qualified to serve the Empire as a District Magistrate. But through the encouragement of his Uncle, he made yet another journey, this time to the Empire's Capital of Ch'ang-an. There he sat for the highly contested Court Examination in the presence of the august Tai Zong, Emperor of the Tang Dynasty.

Quan Wu-Meng was by this time twenty-nine years old and after more then ten years of seemingly endless study, he was awarded the prestigious title of "The Finished Scholar".

It was possible that he would be awarded a much-sought-after and acclaimed post at the Hanlin Academy, where all the Empire's Judiciary System and Laws were reviewed and accessed. But he wanted to begin at the district level. Here, as Magistrate, he could be most effective in weeding out corrupt officials and criminals. He swore to bring such vile elements to justice. No-one under his jurisdiction would suffer the same fate as his parents. There would be peace and justice for all the people he was sent to govern.

While in the Capital, he was fortunate to enjoy the friendship of the great Elder Soong Fu-Liu, the Emperor's principal adviser. Soong was highly respected for his intimate and detailed knowledge of the Empire, having spent a lifetime as a reformist of the Judiciary system of which Quan Wu-Meng was now a by-product. It was Soong whom Quan approached for a district posting and who assigned him to the Sui-chou District where he would serve as Magistrate.

On Judge Quan's departure from the Capital to his post, Elder Soong advised the young and inexperienced man thus:

"Be wise; be diligent; for the Empire is vast and grand. Value those who are your friends; be vigilant against those who are not."

Judge Quan shifted uneasily behind his desk and reflected on the people he had been placed to govern. For the first five days, there had been what seemed to be an endless round of greetings and banquets held in his honour. One banquet in particular was hosted by the town's Hotel Guild-Master, Sheng Lu-ching. An oversized and eccentric figure who loved to recite poems in the midst of a drinking spree, he was nonetheless a powerful person; a shrewd and intelligent businessman who now owned three of the largest hotels in town. Though the Judge loathed such pompous and time-wasting celebrations, he knew that he must not offend such a reputable figure.

The Judge was surprised to learn that one of the guests, Candidate Soong, was the only son of Elder Soong. The young man had the same confident and impressive stature as his father and he had attained high marks in his Judiciary entry exam. The Judge noticed, however, that he seemed to be somewhat nervous and reserved. Perhaps the constant flow of wine had affected the boy. Judge Quan couldn't help but sense that he had been given this post by Elder Soong in order to keep a close watch on his son's progress.

The Judge directed his attention back to the present. The Tribunal library was spacious and elegantly decorated. The large red wooden desk had various intricate carvings, one in particular being a long dragon intertwined around the edges of the desk. Its feet rested on clouds high above the ground. Fire streamed from the dragon's mouth, as it stood defiantly against all adversities. This dragon was a symbol of the power and authority that had been bestowed upon the bearer of the Tribunal seal, the Magistrate himself. Behind him were two large porcelain vases and between them hung a large painting of mountains, symbolizing grandeur and endurance.

He looked at the dozen or so scrolls stacked on a chair next to the table. They showed the current condition of the town. Detailed figures on population, housing, births, marriages and deaths were all listed. Others contained details of taxes that had been collected. Yet others included descriptions of recent cases of theft and property boundary disputes.

All in all, the Judge thought that his predecessor had left this jurisdiction in extremely good order. Contrary to the Capital's view, the people appeared to be abiding by the law; they were prosperous and they paid their taxes on time. Each important legal document had been checked and stored neatly in the Tribunal archives. All disputes had been dealt with in an orderly and prompt manner. In a way, the Judge regretted that all was well. He would rather have had one or two challenging criminal cases to await his resolution.

He gave a deep sigh, stood up and looked down. He wore a grey loose tunic with a cloth band around his waist; his white loose trousers underneath the tunic gave him freedom of movement and would be comfortable in the hot sultry weather that was bound to make itself felt as the morning progressed. Indeed, the Judge looked more like a commoner then a District Magistrate.

He felt the need to escape from the four walls of this Tribunal library. Though it was large and comfortable, his service lay with the people and it was there that he must observe and learn about their daily lives and habits, so as better to provide for them and serve them.

Quietly and without hesitation, the Judge slipped out of the Tribunal's back entrance unannounced. He walked briskly to his left, then turned the corner and walked alongside the high Tribunal walls towards the front entrance. There the Judge continued along the path that would lead him to the town's market-place, confident that his unassuming attire and brisk gait would allow him to visit the town *incognito*.

Although it was still early morning, the long, straight street was already bustling with numerous farmers bringing in their produce by wheelbarrow or cart. Street side stalls with puppeteers, fortune-tellers and barbers were also preparing themselves for a busy day's work.

Judge Quan stood underneath a tall and grand archway placed across the street. Its four tall red pillars were each supported by a block of square stone decorated by a number of painted golden squares and enhanced by a wrapping of red silk. The stone was complemented by a grand yellow-tiled sloping roof, reminiscent of the Grand Palace in the Capital. This was no ordinary archway, thought the Judge; the people believed that such a structure served the purpose of blocking the path of any and all malevolent ghosts. Without freedom of travel within the town, it was thought that such ghosts would become frustrated and leave the town and the people in peace.

Underneath the archway, the Judge observed a beggar walking past, soliciting his daily needs. Another beggar, dressed in torn dirty clothes, carried a large dirty cloth bag in which lay all his belongings. This second beggar, wearing an old hat with chicken feathers protruding from the sides, walked unassumingly into one of the hotels owned by the town's Hotel Guild-Master. The hotel caretaker saw who was coming and quickly ran from behind his counter at the hotel entrance to block the beggar's path. One hand clutched his nose to repel the beggar's obnoxious smell and the other hand waved for the beggar to leave. This beggar, well learned in his arts, began to scream and to clap two small sticks in his hands while reciting a self-composed poem. It was an unwelcome commotion for the early morning guests of the hotel and the caretaker had no choice but to hand some money and food to the intruder. The beggar accepted the gifts immediately, walked out of the hotel and stuck a red paper at the entrance to serve as a warning for other beggars to stay away and leave the hotel and its caretaker in peace, at least for a few days.

Judge Quan smiled and walked along the street, amazed at the resilience of the people. He eventually found himself outside a small temple dedicated to Lord Guan, better known as the "Military Sage". People would normally come and pay their respects early in the morning; some would come to have their illnesses cured while others would seek fortune-tellers within the temple courtyard.

The Judge walked into the temple and saw that a fortune-teller had written a character on a yellow piece of paper as a charm. Its final elongated stroke was supposed to represent a lightning bolt, from which came Heaven and Earth, disrupting primeval chaos and darkness. Lightning had a special significance as it transformed chaos into order. Judge Quan knew that this paper would be pasted on a door to ward off evil.

Another fortune-teller was consulting a large red book. Quan smiled to himself for he knew that this was an Almanac devised and approved yearly by the Emperor. The book contained various seasonal details that would assist agriculture. Through this book, the Emperor showed he was the "Son of Heaven".

This particular fortune-teller had his customer utter three words. Each character was then broken down into a number of strokes from which all the strokes were tallied to form a single number. Twenty-four pages of charts in the Almanac were then consulted; each chart leading to another, until a final chart was reached. From this was derived a collective message, allowing the fortune-teller to interpret his customer's three uttered words with Heaven's blessing.

Musing over what he had seen, Judge Quan eventually turned and left the temple. On his way back to the Tribunal, he told himself that he was unsure of the Almanac's divination qualities, even though he knew that the book was regarded as professing the Emperor's rule. The people of the town who consulted this book proved to him that they had faith in the Emperor's rule and therefore were abiding by his law. It seemed, to the Judge's regret, that, in such a law-abiding place, he might be relegated to the tasks of administration only. There was nothing in the town that was of major interest to him.

CHAPTER TWO

Anyone who has worked long and hard under the hot sun
should rightly expect to reap the rewards of their efforts.
To steal is blatantly to take away that just reward
and that person's pride and joy.

The continuous beat of a Tribunal drum outside the main gate signalled to the town that the morning court session would begin soon. Judge Quan was already adorned in his black Magistrate's robe, with the intricate square embroidery of a large Phoenix marking the Judge's rank as District Magistrate and holder of the "Finished Scholar" title. It was a proud and resplendent figure who stood before the people of Sui-chou and presided over his first court session.

Quan approached the raised dais and took his seat behind a large bench draped with a long red silk cloth. On the left of the bench were the Magistrate's seal of office, several writing brushes, an ink-stone and many scrolls of court documents. To his right was a cylindrical holder that contained numerous long bamboo sticks with numbers painted on them. They were used to indicate the number of strokes an accused would receive during a punishment.

The Tribunal's scribe sat behind a small wooden desk below the dais, to the Judge's right. He was responsible for recording accurately all activities in court. Such records were then used as evidence and would subsequently be sent to the Regional Prefecture to pass sentence on an accused.

To the front and on both sides of Judge Quan were two large pillars painted red, one displaying the insignia of Heaven and the other the insignia of Earth. Directly in front stood two rows of Tribunal officers, each wearing a one-piece grey tunic, the pair of trousers underneath the tunic allowing them freedom of movement. It was they who would carry out the various orders of the Judge and ensure that all court rules were adhered to. To the accused they were the dreaded "Punishers" who enforced the various torture methods necessary to bring a suspect to confess his or her crime. Although as individuals they looked less imposing then the Magistrate, as a collective group with their long curved swords strapped around their waists, they were a frightening sight for any accused persons brought before the court.

Judge Quan surveyed the courtroom and estimated that there were only eight or so townspeople in attendance, no doubt a small, curious crowd, here to see how their new Magistrate would perform. Satisfied that all was in order, Judge Quan rapped a rectangular wooden gavel hard against the bench and announced in a loud clear voice that the morning court session had commenced.

A Tribunal clerk approached the bench with a long, white scroll in both his hands. As he faced the dais, he lowered his head to the Judge and gently handed the scroll to him. Judge Quan took his time silently reading the scroll. Then he lifted his head, smiled and announced in a clear and audible voice that the complainant Siu should be brought before the bench.

Soon an elderly woman was brought into the courtroom and was assisted by an officer to kneel in front of the Judge. Her dark blue outfit, old and torn in many places, indicated that she was a farmer's wife. After she had bowed to the Judge and lifted her head, the Judge could see that there were tears in her eyes.

"Mrs Siu, I shall now read aloud your complaint to this Tribunal yesterday regarding the theft of your vegetable crop." The Judge looked at Mrs Siu and then read the complaint aloud as follows: "'This insignificant person's name is Siu and her first name is Lu-ming. I'm an old and tired farmer's widow. My husband passed away suddenly and Heaven did not bless us with any children. I tried to make ends meet by continuing to farm, but lately, someone has been stealing the crop the day before I was going to harvest it. I beg Your Honour to find the thieves and bring them to justice.'"

Judge Quan finished reading Mrs Siu's complaint, looked up at the court, and announced, "As of today, I pronounce the case of Siu resolved and complete. Bring in the accused right now!"

The complainant Siu, and the people in the crowd were amazed at how fast the case had been resolved. All looked intently at the Judge in anticipation and bewilderment. The prison warden brought a middle-aged man into the court and pushed the accused onto the floor. As he fell, the man bowed continuously to the Judge, crying aloud that an injustice had been done to him, "I am innocent. I have done nothing wrong. I am just a poor farmer...."

An officer hit the man's head with the handle of his sword and immediately the man became quiet. Anyone who stood in front of the Judge could speak only if directed to do so by the Magistrate himself. Judge Quan remained patient and finally invited the man to speak.

"This person's surname is Yan and his first name is Li-Shing. I was minding my own business selling vegetables at the local market when these two officers arrested me and dragged me to court without any reason. I beg your honour, I am a law-abiding citizen and I've done no wrong now or in the past. Please, Your Honour."

Complainant Siu looked at the accused and immediately recognized her friendly neighbour farmer, a good friend of her late husband. She looked at the Judge as if to indicate that he had caught the wrong person. At the same time, an officer handed the Judge some vegetables found on the accused's market stall.

"Silence, you insolent fool! Last night I ordered an officer to Siu's property and instructed him to scribe, in the smallest of characters, the name, Siu, on the leaves of twenty vegetable plants. This morning, two officers went to the local market stall and checked who was in possession of the specially-marked vegetables. They found all twenty at your stall."

Judge Quan stood up and in a rage threw the specially marked plants towards the accused. As they landed in front of Yan, the tiny words were easily visible to him.

"You dare to lie in court to your Magistrate? Speak the truth now or this court will confiscate your property?"

Yan was clearly frightened. The Judge's finger pointed straight at him and the two wings of the Judge's hat shook as he clearly showed his anger.

The accused Yan looked away from the Judge and then at the vegetables in front of him. Frightened, and unable to think clearly, he had no choice but immediately to confess to his crime. He bowed low and gave a detailed and tearful confession which the court scribe recorded. As Yan ended with a plea for forgiveness, the scribe handed the written confession to the Judge. Judge Quan read the full confession aloud to Yan and to the court. At the end, Yan acknowledged what the Judge had read was accurate and the truth.

Judge Quan continued, "Anyone who has worked long and hard under the hot sun should rightly expect to reap the rewards of their efforts. To steal is blatantly to take away that just reward and that person's pride and joy.

"This is a serious crime and this court passes the sentence of fifty strokes on the thief, Yan. However, since he has admitted to his crime and has therefore saved the court much time and unnecessary effort, it is hereby commuted to twenty strokes."

When he had finished announcing the sentence, Judge Quan took a small red bamboo stick marked with the number twenty and threw it down onto the floor as two officers dragged Yan closer towards the bench, pulling his trousers down and revealing his buttocks. One officer held Yan while the other grabbed a long narrow bamboo batton and proceeded to beat Yan for his crime.

The persons in the court spoke amongst themselves and agreed how clever their new Judge had been in bringing a prompt resolution to the crime. Judge Quan observed their reactions and knew that this case would be talked about in the town for some days to come. He knew that the people were watching his every move and his every decision. The August Moon had indicated to the Judge that the people's prosperity was due to a just Judiciary system. For that reason, the Judge's performance came under close scrutiny by the people he was placed to rule over.

Judge Quan dismissed the complainant, Siu, with some kind words. He then warned Yan that if he offended again he would be stripped of his rights to his land and those rights would be awarded to his victim. Yan would also suffer the public humiliation of bearing a cangue – a large wooden collar – around his neck, and of having both hands bound to the collar. In such a state, he would be obliged to beg on the streets for his food for three months. Yan was frightened out of his wits. He immediately bowed low to the Judge and promised that, from that day onwards, he would be a law-abiding citizen. With his buttocks painful and tender from the beating, Yan was allowed to leave the courtroom.

Revenge from Beyond

With a deep sigh, Judge Quan unrolled another scroll and begun to read, while at the same time caressing his short pointed beard with his right hand. It took quite some time before Judge Quan looked up at the small crowd in the courtroom and begun to announce various new projects to improve the town's sanitation and the health of the people. As he finished his announcements, much to the delight of the people, he reached for his wooden gavel and was about to close the morning session when there was a loud commotion outside the Tribunal. A young woman dressed in a long white gown with red loose sleeves led a large procession of people behind her as she cried and beat her chest, announcing in a loud wailing voice that her husband had been murdered.

Judge Quan noticed that she walked with a slight swaying movement as she approached the bench and knelt before him. At a closer distance, he observed that her white and red dress had intricate red embroidery running all along the seams. Her smooth pale skin was accentuated by long straight hair tied neatly behind her with what appeared to be a red hair-pin in the shape of a peacock. She looked at the Judge with tearful eyes and than turned and looked away from him, at the same time covering her face with her long fluted sleeves. Then she began to cry even louder.

Judge Quan estimated that the young woman could not have been more then twenty years of age. There was a peculiar *redness* about her, Judge Quan remarked to himself, as he encouraged the young lady to speak.

She looked back at the Judge again and with a gentle and quavering voice she begun to address the Magistrate. "This insignificant person's name is Chu, given name Hong-li. My husband Chu Fan-shing and I ran an art gallery from our modest home. Although his art work was not widely accepted, I always believed in his abilities. To make ends meet, I also conducted dancing and singing classes for young girls.

"This morning, when I woke up in our bed, I felt that his body next to mine was unusually cold. His face was still turned towards the wall as I patted him to wake him from his sleep. His body was stiff! I looked at his face; it was dark and purple in colour. Then I saw his eyes...."

21

She looked away and cried. It took some time before Mrs Chu could compose herself once more and than she continued in a low voice, "My husband's eyes were large and bulging out from their cavities. I couldn't look at him any longer. He wasn't asleep; he was dead, and he was gone. What am I to do now that he is dead? What am I to do?"

Mrs Chu's loud wailing cry echoed inside the courtroom as she knelt on the floor and thumped her chest in anguish. The room, in which there were at first just a handful of people, now overflowed with the curious and the disturbed. They murmured amongst themselves and wondered if a crime had been committed. As Mrs Chu's cries became even louder, the people grieved along with her.

Judge Quan quickly reflected on the situation before him. His wish for a more challenging case had now been answered. A young lady was left alone in this suffering world. At such a young age, what would become of her in the future, the Judge thought? He shook his head and with a solemn voice, he began to speak. "I, Magistrate of Sui-chou, will investigate your husband's death and see that justice is done."

The Judge ordered the court officers to prepare his palanquin so that he might proceed to the Chu residence immediately. He then rapped his desk with the gavel and ended the morning court session.

The people in the courtroom filed out slowly, discussing amongst themselves what had just transpired. What bad omen had this new Magistrate brought with him to this previously quiet and peaceful town, now alarmed by the death of a well-known artist? Why didn't the Judge ask Mrs Chu for more information? Could it be that the Judge was still inexperienced or could it be that he knew more about the case than the people had been led to believe?

CHAPTER THREE

*Judge Quan's lack of experience and attraction
to the young widow Chu could severely jeopardize
the resolution of this suspected murder case.*

A large and curious crowd had already gathered outside the
Tribunal's main gate. Word was out about the death at Mrs
Chu's residence and the crowds were there to catch a glimpse of
their Judge. The palanquin, barely large enough for two, was
placed directly in front of the Tribunal staircase. Two officers
stood at the front and two more at the rear of the palanquin to
guard and protect the Judge. A further two officers carried the
large orange and yellow Tribunal banner and led the procession.

Judge Quan appeared above on the staircase and walked
briskly down before entering his palanquin, stopping for a
moment to catch a glimpse of the sun. It was directly above in
the sky and the hot sultry air made him feel uncomfortable in his
thick, dark Magistrate's robe.

The crowd begun to move along with the procession as the
palanquin wound its way towards the Chu residence. It was not
long before it crossed the bridge over the river and revealed the
more scenic part of the town. There were numerous willow trees
and rock formations. Lovers and poets, inspired by the beauty of
this spot, had often composed and inscribed their poems there.
Nearby was a large hotel owned by Sheng Lu-ching, the Hotel
Guild-Master. For a moment, Judge Quan thought he caught a
glimpse of Candidate Soong at the hotel tea-house.

The procession wound its way through the farming sector and
then turned northward towards the Chu residence. From afar,
Judge Quan could see the type of house that Mrs Chu lived in.
The houses were mainly double-storied and looked quite opulent
as they glittered underneath the sunshine. But as the procession
approached the houses, he could see they were made mainly of
wood, filled in with a mixture of clay and straw. The exteriors
were grey and the roofs were made mainly from wood and
ceramic tiles.

They continued along numerous narrow streets, marred by
garbage and filth piled up at the roadside, and exposed to the hot
sun. Judge Quan reflected that these houses were less then

23

opulent. The region had once been occupied by well-to-do citizens but an uprising by the poor had caused the Judge of the day to allow these people to settle here as an act of appeasement.

When the procession arrived at the Chu residence, Judge Quan wasted no time leaving the palanquin and striding into the courtyard. He was greeted at the door by a grieving Mrs Chu and the local Warden, Xu. Looking at the Warden, Judge Quan barked at him.

"You incompetent snake! Why didn't you post a guard outside the residence? The crime scene and any evidence may have been tampered with. What were you doing all this time?"

"Yes, but I wasn't told to...."

"You shouldn't need to be told. It's done in every crime scene, you dog-head!" Judge Quan then immediately posted two guards outside the gate. Leaving Warden Xu kneeling on the ground, he walked across the small courtyard and entered the house, with Mrs Chu following closely behind.

The Judge entered a small reception hall, lightly decorated with a few paintings, a reception desk and the customary tea-table and chair. No doubt this was where Fan-shing had discussed his paintings with potential buyers. Although the room lacked any expensive decorations, what little the Chus had was exquisitely displayed.

A door at the rear of the reception room led to the gallery. Judge Quan moved closer to inspect each painting and realized why Fan-shing's paintings had not been widely accepted. The brush-strokes were not refined and the use of colours was not consistent, failing to blend in with the painting as a whole. Consequently, there was no harmony among people, animals and nature, as was desirable in works of art.

Judge Quan caught a slight scent of perfume from behind him and realized Mrs Chu's presence. He turned and spoke to her. "As students of the Judiciary system, all Candidates are encouraged and indeed tested in their knowledge of arts, poetry and medicine. These are regarded not only as essential knowledge but deemed necessary to promote harmony of thinking and spirit. The Candidate is encouraged to link such qualities to his tasks as Magistrate of the people. I notice that your late husband's work represents a new artistic style. The main emphasis is on the artist's mood at the time the painting was done. This is in contrast to expressions from the heart that represent poetic and romantic settings."

Mrs Chu looked at the Judge and then politely bowed and replied, "Indeed my husband was from the new school. He was always a passionate man, a man full of energy and spontaneity. I know that such a style suited his nature, and as you have seen, Your Honour, his paintings were full of life, joy and, I guess, sorrow." Mrs Chu looked down at the floor in silence.

Judge Quan disliked such expressions. He felt that they were far from harmonious and indeed not conducive to the improvement of the human spirit as a whole. However, he looked at the sorrowful Mrs Chu as if touched by the legacy of her husband's work.

Mrs Chu eased past the Judge and directed him up the stairs to where the bedroom was situated. It was only then that he noticed that Mrs Chu was already wearing a white mourning dress, her small steps and somewhat sensual movements indicating that she was probably skilful in the ancient art of folk dancing.

Moving towards the staircase, Mrs Chu took the Judge past Fan-shing's workshop, which was situated next to the gallery with only a thin wall separating the two rooms. Judge Quan stopped to examine some of Fan-shing's unfinished paintings. Here were all the customary paints, brushes, canvasses and figurines used by an artist.

What caught the Judge's attention was a painting that appeared to be near completion, left on a stand in the middle of the workshop. He moved closer to examine the work, but Mrs Chu interrupted from behind with her low soft voice.

"My husband worked night and day on this. He would often sell his paintings to repay his gambling debts. I cannot imagine how much he must have owed to have worked so fervently on this." She looked away from the Judge, seemingly with tears in her eyes.

Judge Quan moved closer to the painting. He noted that the brush-strokes were much more refined than in all the artist's previous paintings. Each stroke blended effortlessly with the next as if elegantly drawn by one long stroke. Here were all the characteristics of the old school of art, unlike Fan Shing's previous works. It was, Judge Quan thought, highly unusual that a person should switch from one style to another so suddenly.

"Your husband showed considerable talent in his ability to adapt to two forms of art," he said.

"Without any doubt, Your Honour, he was a man of many talents. In this instance, I can only guess that he painted in the style requested by a customer," Mrs Chu replied, looking towards, but not directly at, the Judge.

"Interesting!" the Judge said to Mrs Chu, as he politely asked to be taken to the bedroom.

Judge Quan pitied the woman, widowed at such a young age. As Magistrate, he himself had consistently refused to enter into a marriage. He must first and foremost serve the people, and it would take all his time and effort to do so. Furthermore, his work was tiring and dangerous. It would not be fair to a wife if anything untoward were to happen to him.

Mrs Chu took Judge Quan to the kitchen at the back of the house. Judge Quan noted that there was only one dining-chair. When she saw the Judge's bewildered look, she said, "My husband spent most of his time in tea-houses, losing all our money. When I chided him, he just said that they were excellent places in which to find prospective buyers for his paintings."

Judge Quan nodded and admired Mrs Chu's lack of complaint about what must have been a difficult marriage.

After accompanying the Judge to another back room, where, as she said, she conducted her folklore, dance and singing classes, she then led him to a bedroom on the second floor. As the Judge climbed the staircase with the woman behind him, he quickly motioned for two Tribunal officers to follow them up to the second floor.

They walked along a short corridor towards the bedroom where Fan-shing's body still lay. Suddenly, Mrs Chu stumbled into Judge Quan and fell towards the floor. She would have hit her head, were it not that Judge Quan managed to hold her arm in time.

"Where is the Coroner?" asked the Judge. The two officers looked at each other, bewildered. The Judge was furious and was about to snap at his men when he realized that it was he who was at fault. This was his first possible murder case and, preoccupied by the inspection of Fan-shing's paintings, he had forgotten to give explicit instructions for a Coroner to be summoned. He immediately gave orders to an officer to fetch the Coroner. The other officer was to stay with Mrs Chu until the Coroner arrived. The Judge would proceed to inspect the bedroom by himself.

He entered the bedroom and immediately noticed that Fang-Shing's body still lay on the bed with his back towards the Judge. Relieved that the room appeared not to have been tampered with, the Judge quickly walked over to the raised, wooden bed.

Fan Shing's swollen body was lying against the wall, leaving only the left side of his face visible to the Judge. The eyes and mouth were open and the skin was a dull purple colour. The same colour affected the hands and feet. Unable to see the mouth and nose, the Judge could not detect any visible signs of external bleeding.

Taking care not to move or disturb the body, he moved the back of his right hand over the entire length of the corpse. The body felt cool and the Judge realized that Fan-shing must have died in the late hours of the previous night.

The artist's light grey tunic was still intact, as was the white blanket which only partially covered the upper body. Fang-shing appeared to sleep on the inside of the bed, quite unusual as females usually slept on that side. His neck still rested on a long wooden block, which acted as a pillow. The Judge looked at the blanket and the white bed-sheets; they all appeared to be in good order, showing no signs of a struggle.

Judge Quan looked to his left and noticed the window; he walked over and examined the wooden sill and the paper covering the wooden square lattice. All were intact and there was no indication of tampering or forced entry.

He turned to face the middle of the room and looked at the roof above him. The tiling appeared in good order, as did the dark wooden beams underneath the tiles. Four of these beams held up a half-ceiling at the back of the room, forming a spacious cock-loft. This was being used to store various items such as reed mats and clothes. The bed lay to the rear of the room, opposite the entrance. All in all, Judge Quan was perplexed as to how a murderer could have gained entry and killed Fang-Shing without the victim struggling against the attacker. At the same time, how could Mrs Chu have remained sound asleep?

Puzzled, Judge Quan scratched his head as again he looked round the room and spotted several low cupboards situated next to the wall opposite the window. He walked over to the cupboards, inside of which were various combs, pins and, in particular, the red hairpin Mrs Chu wore during the morning court session when she reported her husband's murder.

"That was a gift from my husband for my last birthday. It is still my favourite pin."

Seeing her husband's body, Mrs Chu lifted her long white sleeves over her head and began to weep. Judge Quan quickly led her out of the room and away from the body. When he entered the corridor, he was met by a middle-aged man carrying a large bag over his shoulders. Upon seeing the Judge, the man bowed his head and introduced himself.

"This insignificant person's surname is Chen, given name Tsu-wee. I practice herbal medicine and operate a shop in this town. For the past five years, I have been the town's Coroner working in conjunction with your Honorable predecessor."

Inadvertently, the Judge had placed one arm around Mrs Chu to support her. She quickly took a step back, embarrassed by his display of sympathy for her. Looking annoyed and somewhat embarrassed also, the Judge then turned and looked at the Coroner, estimating that the man would be in his late fifties. His hair was grey with numerous white streaks and his deep facial lines were partially covered by a long white beard.

Judge Quan smiled and stepped forward respectfully to raise Coroner Chen's shoulders, "You are more advanced in age and have more years of experience than I have, so let's do away with any formalities since we will be working together."

To himself, the Judge admitted quietly that this Coroner bore a resemblance to his own Uncle.

Following this brief introduction, the Judge asked the Coroner to inspect the room closely and gather all necessary evidence for the case. He also instructed an officer to organize an afternoon court session in the courtyard of the Chu residence. The Judge then placed the second officer outside the bedroom to ensure no other person was allowed inside the room while the Coroner was performing his investigations. Judge Quan himself accompanied the grief-stricken Mrs Chu down the stairs and back to Fan-shing's workshop, where he hoped again to inspect Fan-shing's last painting.

Coroner Chen began his work by examining the deceased's body. He could not understand why the Judge was not in the room to conduct the investigation with him. He gave a loud sigh, thinking that the Judge's predecessor would have done things differently. The Judge's lack of experience and attraction to the young widow Chu could severely jeopardize the resolution of this suspected murder case.

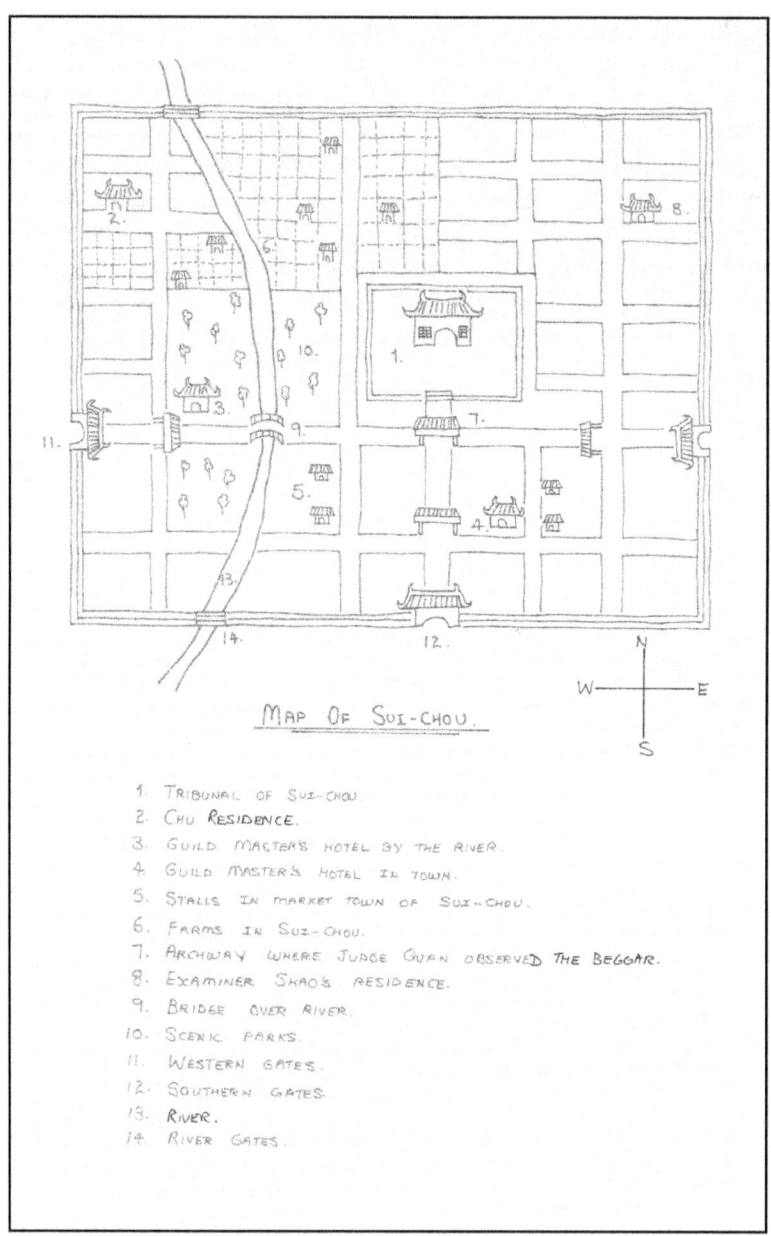

MAP OF SUI-CHOU.

1. TRIBUNAL OF SUI-CHOU
2. CHU RESIDENCE.
3. GUILD MASTER'S HOTEL BY THE RIVER.
4. GUILD MASTER'S HOTEL IN TOWN.
5. STALLS IN MARKET TOWN OF SUI-CHOU.
6. FARMS IN SUI-CHOU.
7. ARCHWAY WHERE JUDGE OUAN OBSERVED THE BEGGAR.
8. EXAMINER SHAO'S RESIDENCE.
9. BRIDGE OVER RIVER.
10. SCENIC PARKS.
11. WESTERN GATES.
12. SOUTHERN GATES.
13. RIVER.
14. RIVER GATES.

Map Of Sui-Chou

CHAPTER FOUR

The people believed a victim's soul would linger close to his
body, especially after a sudden and untimely death.
Having been cheated of life, the soul would quickly
posess the body of any innocent passer-by
in the hope of continuing his life and avenging his death.

A makeshift Tribunal was temporarily erected in the courtyard of the Chu residence. Judge Quan sat behind a desk and on a chair borrowed from the reception area. A large table was placed directly in front of the Judge. On this, the body of Fan-shing had been laid. Coroner Chen prepared two tubs of warm water, unfolded some new white clothes and took out various implements from his bag. He then took up a position next to the deceased while Mrs Chu stood to the Judge's left, behind her husband's body.

Judge Quan noticed for the first time that the courtyard was small by any standard. But, despite its size, it was decorated by a large willow tree in the centre and numerous pot-plants had been placed around the tree, as well as in various parts of the yard. In these tranquil surroundings, the Judge regretted that such an aesthetic scene would be disturbed by the macabre task of examining a victim's body.

With a deep sigh of regret, Judge Quan announced in a loud voice that the afternoon court session would commence. "Upon the discovery of her husband's death," he announced, "Mrs Chu Hong-li quickly reported the suspected murder to the Tribunal. This Tribunal in turn has acted swiftly to investigate the possible crime by securing the scene and conducting a thorough search of the premises. To date, no unusual weapons or poison have been found. It is therefore imperative for the Tribunal to conduct a thorough examination of the deceased's body. Perhaps the clue to the murder lies within. I have therefore instructed the Coroner to begin his examination of Chu Fan-shing's body."

Judge Quan gave the signal to Coroner Chen to begin and focussed his attention on the Coroner's every word and movement. The Tribunal scribe also listened intently, ready to record every word that the Coroner spoke. Coroner Chen asked Mrs Chu to identify the corpse. Reluctantly she walked closer and peered at the naked and swollen body of her husband. Then she nodded, turned and tearfully walked back. The Coroner washed his hands in a tub of water placed next to the previously-washed and now dry corpse. He opened a small pot and extracted some boiled vinegar using a cloth wrapped around a bamboo stick. With the stick, he wiped the whole body quickly with the vinegar. Then he sprinkled some brown rice over the body and proceeded to cover it, allowing some time for the vinegar and rice grain to soften the body's skin and eventually reveal any signs of mortal wounds, however small.

While allowing time for the vinegar to react, Coroner Chen began to prepare several implements, including a silver needle. He then boiled some glutinous rice in another pot. After the rice began to boil, he uncovered the corpse and proceeded to wash all the vinegar and rice away with water from the second tub.

When he had finished the washing, he immediately began to inspect the corpse's head. Then he proceeded to examine the ears, the nose, and the face, all the while searching for any signs of penetration made by a knife or needle. – Any mortal blows made days earlier would have resulted in a progressive deterioration and would also have appeared as discoloured spots. – As he worked, he systematically recorded his observations on a piece of paper. He then turned the body over and continued his examination, much to the agitation of Mrs Chu, for she had to witness the unceremonious inspection of her husband's naked body. The Judge, however, was very impressed by the thoroughness of the Coroner's examination and his attention to detail.

After a while, the Coroner made his report, as follows. "The deceased is a man in his late thirties, already identified by his wife as Chu Fan-shing. From the stiffness and initial coldness of the body, I surmise that the victim must have died early this morning. I have made a thorough examination of the body and have not found any evidence of wounds inflicted by burns, sharp objects or blows to the body. I have yet to consider death by poison – that will be my next examination – but I surmise that the victim died a sudden and painful death."

"How did you come to that conclusion, Coroner, since there are no visible signs of any wounds?" the Judge asked, bewildered.

"The whole body appears tense. The left arm seems to be reaching in the direction of his neck; the mouth is slightly open, while the right hand is closed tightly. It appears that he was struggling for air."

Judge Quan could not believe that he had missed such obvious and important observations. Such clues could prove critical in the investigation and, as Judge, he should not have overlooked the signs detected by Coroner Chen. As he remembered it now, he had in fact been anxious to look once more at Fan-shing's last painting, but, diverted by Mrs Chu's grief, had chosen to speak to her at length about her folklore, dance and singing classes, which had appeared to calm her.

"Permission to inspect for any poison, Your Honour?" Coroner Chen interrupted Judge Quan's chain of thought. With a wave of the hand, the Judge confirmed that the Coroner could begin an internal examination of the deceased.

The Coroner took the silver needle, dipped it into a solution of lye made from beans and placed it into the deceased's mouth, covering it with several pieces of paper. The Coroner then took an egg, poked it with another needle and allowed the egg white to flow out and into his rice mixture. He then stirred the mixture until the water had almost evaporated.

Judge Quan had read about these forensic procedures before, but had never seen them being demonstrated. He had full admiration for this Coroner. Most would have been satisfied with the detection of poison by using the silver needle method. Coroner Chen was, however, careful to back this method with another, to try to establish beyond any doubt whether poison had been used and, if so, in what form.

Coroner Chen began to remove the paper and the silver needle from the corpse's mouth. The needle had turned dark blue. He placed it back into the lye solution and then took it out again. The dark blue colour remained. He then recorded his findings.

When he had finished, he took the glutinous rice mixture and placed some of its contents into the corpse's mouth, eyes and ears. Once more he sprinkled some brown rice over the body. Then he immersed a large quantity of new cotton wool in the vinegar and covered the body with it. After a few moments, he moved even closer, but immediately stood back as a foul smell arose from the body. Undeterred, he placed one hand over his own mouth and nose and began to remove the now darkened cotton wool. The rice mixture, too, had darkened and had also turned liquid. The Coroner then recorded more of his findings and after quite some time made his final report to the Judge.

"From my examinations, I conclude from the degree and nature of the colouration of the silver needle, along with the rice mixture method, that the deceased, Chu Fan-shing, died from White Powder poison.

"This poison is usually made from a harmless herb found within the mountain region outside of this town. Mixed with a series of other herbs and in certain quantities, it forms a potent poison. If diffused in the body's blood-stream, it quickly attacks the victim's throat and this explains why the deceased died quietly and appeared to be gasping for air. The poison also attacks the brain so that death comes almost instantaneously. This explains the lack of a struggle."

Hearing that Fan-shing had died from White Powder poison, there were numerous murmurs amongst the spectators looking through the opened gate outside the courtyard. Although there was still some space left in the courtyard, no-one dared to venture too close to a victim who had died a sudden death.

Judge Quan looked around the courtyard and then at the people standing outside. He knew that the people believed that a victim's soul would linger close to his body, especially after a sudden and untimely death. Having been cheated of life, the soul would quickly possess the body of any innocent passer-by in the hope of continuing his life and avenging his death. Only those who could write were protected, as it was believed that written characters possess special powers to dispel any lingering souls or ghosts. Judge Quan knew that such were the superstitions of the people. He returned his attention back to Coroner Chen. "How was the poison introduced?" he asked.

"By way of inhalation. The poison could be administered either through food or through the air. In this case, I found a large quantity of the substance in the victim's nose and throat."

Impressed, Judge Quan asked the scribe to read aloud the Coroner's findings. After this had been done, Coroner Chen agreed that the scribe's account was accurate. He then walked towards the scribe and took out a small, rectangular, marbled stone with his own name inscribed at the bottom. He inked the bottom of the stone and pressed it firmly against the written scroll, thereby adding his seal to the document. He then stamped the notes he had taken during his examination and passed these to the Tribunal's scribe.

Mrs Chu fell to her knees and bowed profusely to the Judge. She urged that her husband's murderer be found and said that, without justice, his soul would linger indefinitely over the town, haunting it, searching for his murderer and his own form of justice.

Revenge from Beyond

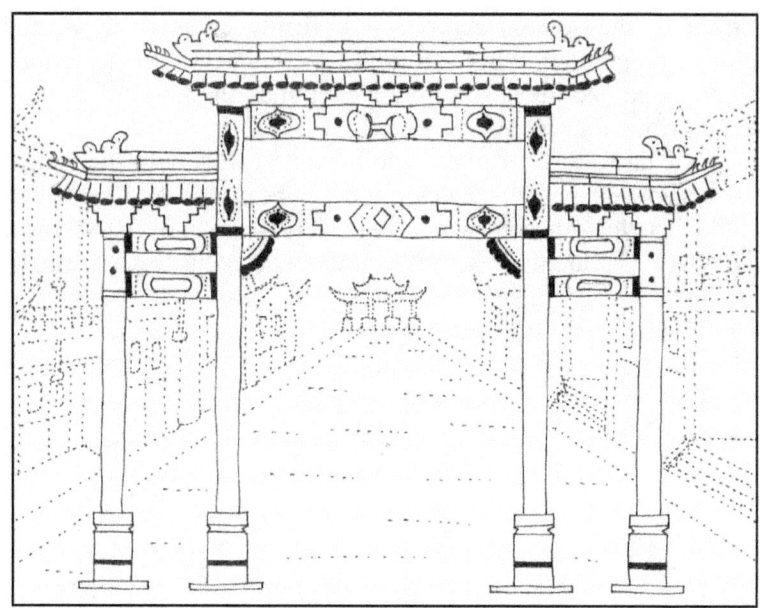

Grand Archway at the Town Marketplace.

Judge Quan, Coroner Chen and E-Lung Discuss New Developments in the Tribunal Library. Fan Shing's Painting is near the Window.

i

CHAPTER FIVE

I know, through many years of experience,
that she is a wicked person.
In one day she managed to attract the whole crowd to her side
and I am afraid that she has also caught Your Honour's eye.

Judge Quan sat there, astonished at Mrs Chu's fearful and earnest speech. He looked at the agitated people outside the courtyard, noting that some had run away from the scene, fearful of a ghost and a murderer at large in their own town.

The Judge sat, apparently impassive, and spoke to the people inside and outside the courtyard. "The Tribunal of Sui-chou will do its utmost to find this criminal and bring justice to the Chu family. Your Magistrate will not relent as long as a murderer lives and breathes in our town." The Judge paused. His speech was an attempt to bring order and calm the people. Then he continued, "Since the Coroner has now completed his examination, I release the body of Chu Fan-shing to Mrs Chu. She may begin her bereavement and burial proceedings immediately."

Then Judge Quan slammed his fist against the table so hard that even Mrs Chu stopped her crying and bowed reverently.

The Judge ordered the room where Fan-shing's body was found to be sealed and made off-limits to all people, including Mrs Chu. He also ordered the last unfinished painting to be brought to the Tribunal as evidence in the murder case. He then suggested that Mrs Chu might stay with friends during the investigation, or if this was not possible, a suitable lodging in the Tribunal's compound could be found for her.

Mrs Chu bowed once more to the Judge for his kind offer. "This insignificant person is now in a state of mourning for her husband and would think it appropriate to do so right here at her home." Judge Quan nodded in approval. "As for my husband's last painting, I beg the Magistrate not to take it away. Please let my husband's soul linger amongst his paintings so that at the time of his burial, he will leave this world in total peace and contentment."

"I am deeply saddened by the loss of your husband and indeed respect your dedication towards him after his death. What will you do after your husband is buried?" Judge Quan asked

"There is nothing for me here in this town. I must sell this house and Fan-shing's works to pay for his burial. I will then move back to my parents' village. There I will hope to live a quiet and secluded widow's life." Mrs Chu's voice began to quiver as she spoke of the sad and lonely life ahead for her.

"This whole town is full of admiration for your dutiful respect for your late husband," said the Magistrate. "I consent that you may stay in this house to prepare for your husband's funeral. As to the painting, it is the court's evidence and it will be kept safely in the Tribunal during the course of this investigation. I am sure that your husband would have approved of my action."

Mrs Chu was about to protest, but Judge Quan abruptly rapped with his gavel once more. He headed quickly towards the direction of his palanquin, but momentarily stopped to offer Coroner Chen a ride back to his shop in town. The Coroner accepted, and both men headed away from the Chu residence.

Once in the palanquin and sitting opposite the Coroner, Judge Quan expressed his curiosity about the Coroner's examination technique. "If you don't mind my asking, where did you learn the examination techniques you applied to Fan-shing's body?"

"My father taught me the herbalist's trade when I was young. He would often take me deep into the mountains and explain to me the good and bad effects of certain herbs on the human body. I practice what I have learned after many years of dedicated guidance and teaching by my father."

Then Coroner Chen moved closer to Judge Quan and whispered, "Would Your Honour allow me to speak frankly and honestly to you?"

Judge Quan was taken aback by the Coroner's frankness, but agreed, courteously.

"I know I speak out of turn in regard to Your Honour's ability and his dedication to the people of this town. I know Mrs Chu is an elegant, young and beautiful lady. But I also know, through many years of experience, that she is a wicked person. In one day, she managed to attract the whole crowd to her side and I am afraid that she also caught Your Honour's eye."

The Coroner paused while trying to find the correct words to continue.

Judge Quan was furious at the Coroner's insinuation but before he could speak, Coroner Chen boldly cut in. He pointed his finger outside the palanquin and continued to speak. "Look at these people; they are all talking about you. They see you as a father and regard you and your position with the greatest respect. They now have a murderer living amongst them and a Judge who appears to be giving little attention to solving the crime, but is paying more regard to Mrs Chu's well-being."

Coroner Chen looked out of the palanquin and at the people. Judge Quan was angry; but, not having the Coroner's full attention, followed his stare. He observed that numerous people were speaking softly amongst themselves, while some were looking at and then walking away from the passing palanquin, in an apparent show of disgust towrads its occupants.

The judge bit his lip and realized that he had made several wrong moves. Out of concern for Mrs Chu, he had offered her the opportunity of staying in the Tribunal compound. He now knew how the people had interpreted this offer. The same concern had taken the Judge away from performing his proper task at the crime scene. In many ways, he had allowed his emotions to get in the way of the murder investigation.

Coroner Chen continued to stare out of the window; he realized that he had angered the Judge. He knew that the Judge could either solicit his advice or arrest him immediately for slander against a presiding magistrate. Charges of such a nature could see him stripped of his title, all his belongings confiscated, and he himself exiled to a remote part of the Empire. For a short time, the Coroner felt that his destiny was in the hands of this young Judge.

Although the Coroner had accused the Judge wrongly, he had at least had the respect to speak to the Judge frankly. The Judge was angered by the Coroner's and the people's wild accusations but thought that he was partly to blame for their wrong impression of him.

Judge Quan, on the other hand, regarded Coroner Chen's bold speech to him as a sign of strength. It was refreshing to hear honest words spoken by the people around him. "Coroner Chen," he said, "You have been involved with this Tribunal for many years. This court has benefited greatly from your deductive work, meticulous examinations and beneficial advice. I must now impose on you a request to work more closely with the Tribunal."

Coroner Chen turned around and looked at the Judge, greatly relieved.

"I want you to work with me as my Sergeant for the duration of this case", Judge Quan continued. "As my Sergeant, you will be my confidant. We will discuss and work together towards the resolution of the case. You have disapproved of my methods and it will now be your duty through your own words to help and apply your vested skills towards the case."

Coroner Chen was taken aback by Judge Quan's invitation. He felt that only the best qualified men could serve in the position the Judge had offered and believed that he was below that capacity. "I thank the Judge for thinking so highly of me," he began, hesitatingly.

The Judge interrupted the Coroner, "Not at all. Let us do away with all formalities and treat each other equally as friends. I know you need time to consider, but if you have even the slightest inclination to accept my offer, please come to the Tribunal tonight. We have urgent matters to discuss. Your presence would in no way constitute a full acceptance of my offer."

On the way back to town, there was total silence between the two men. Judge Quan contemplated the murder case, while Coroner Chen contemplated his future. Judge Quan's offer weighed heavily on his mind. What was he to do? A few moments ago, he had criticized the Judge for disappointing the people. By not accepting the offer to help a Judge in need and resolve a murder case in town, would he in essence be doing the same, and disappointing the people he had known for so long?

CHAPTER SIX

You see, Fan-shing was used to the newer art-form throughout his life; and suddenly to switch style for his final painting is beyond my comprehension.
Perhaps he intended this painting to stand out amongst his other works. Perhaps he wanted to convey a message?

B ack at the Tribunal, Judge Quan quickly changed into a loose and comfortable outfit. An officer had placed Fan-shing's last painting in the library and the Judge once more felt drawn towards it as he drank a cup of tea. He felt exhausted by the long afternoon's court session and placing his hands and head on the library table, he fell into a deep sleep.

It was a long while before Judge Quan was awakened by a knock at the door. An assistant entered and announced that Coroner Chen had arrived at the Tribunal and had requested an impromptu meeting. Judge Quan stood up from his desk, wiped his eyes in an attempt to awaken fully from his nap, and said he would see the Coroner immediately. As the assistant left, Judge Quan paced around impatiently. Finally, he thought, his first good news of the day had arrived.

Coroner Chen entered the already opened door and immediately bowed his head to the Judge.

Judge Quan stepped forward to stop him. "Coroner Chen, I insist that we do away with all customary formalities. You are now in the service of the court and are my friend. I am greatly in your debt for joining in the investigation of this murder case."

"The debt is mine, Your Honour. For many years now I have felt compelled to get away from the shop and spend more time with the people. Confinement all day in a shop can stifle an old man's mind. Your offer to me is very tempting. It has given me an opportunity to become more involved in the service of the people and to hand over some of my responsibilities in the shop to my very capable nephew. However, Your Honour, I must stress that I can do this only for the duration of this one murder case. Once the case is closed, I wish to step down from this responsibility."

"Of course you may!"

Judge Quan continued to speak while Coroner Chen poured a cup of tea for the Judge, before pouring one for himself. Judge Quan realized that, although he had made Coroner Chen his confidant and a friend, he was after all a Magistrate and some form of formality would still need to be maintained.

"I have taken the liberty of bringing Fan-shing's last painting back to the Tribunal. Somehow, I feel drawn to it, as if the clue to the murder lies somewhere within it."

"It appears to be a normal painting, with the usual brush-strokes and colouration," remarked the Coroner.

"Mrs Chu said that her late husband worked day and night on it as if he felt compelled to finish the painting quickly. I found that rather extraordinary," the Judge replied.

Coroner Chen positioned himself closer to the painting as the Judge sat behind his desk and continued his analysis. "You see, Fan-shing was used to the newer art-form throughout his life and suddenly to switch style for his final painting is beyond my comprehension. Perhaps he intended this painting to stand out amongst his other works. Perhaps he wanted to convey a message?" Judge Quan theorized.

"You mean to say, Your Honour, that Fan-shing knew that someone was threatening him?"

"Fan-shing loved to drink and gamble. Mrs Chu said so herself. But to dedicate himself day and night to this last painting...?" Judge Quan broke off and shook his head, convinced that the painting had some significance in the murder case. "Furthermore," Judge Quan continued, "I tried to get a better look at the painting while you were examining Fan-shing's body in the bedroom. It was Mrs Chu's persistent tears and my fear of her fainting once more that drew me away from the task. Secondly, she also tried to deter me from taking possession of this painting, saying that her husband's soul would not be complete without the presence of all his works."

Coroner Chen now realized why Judge Quan had been unable to attend the examination of Fan-shing's body. He felt ashamed that he had previously accused the Judge of paying more attention to Mrs Chu than to the investigation itself. He turned and bowed to the Judge apologetically.

Judge Quan nodded slightly to the Coroner and smiled. It was their first acknowledgement that they both understood each other.

"That Mrs Chu," the Coroner continued, "appeared to grieve every time Your Honour was homing in on what might have been a clue. She tried to draw the attention and the sympathy of the crowd to her side."

"That's true. It was for this very reason that I decided not to question her for too long when she reported her husband's murder in court this morning. She used her looks and sensuality to draw the crowd and that created an unfortunate atmosphere in the courtroom today." Judge Quan paused, took a sip of tea and then continued, "It was only by luck that a few members of the crowd remained at a distance during your examination of Fan-shing's body. When I attempted to bring this painting to the Tribunal, Mrs Chu immediately protested and tried to encourage the crowd to hear her plea. But many of them had left the scene."

Coroner Chen now took a visitor's chair and placed it next to the Judge. Silently, they both examined the painting. It showed a river meandering through a plain with numerous low-lying trees by its banks. The plain itself, with several scattered rows of trees, gently sloped upwards to form three hills. Where the river narrowed, there appeared to be three horses grazing on lush green grass. In the foreground of the painting, there was a grand pavilion perched on top of a flat look-out position, accessible only by an old wooden bridge. A large tree hung directly over the pavilion and partially blocked what was otherwise a serene and harmonious scene.

Judge Quan and Coroner Chen stared at the painting for a considerable time. But they were unable to gather any clues that might connect it with the murder case. Both men were drawn to the simplicity of the painting and the way that the artist had portrayed nature and men interacting harmoniously together. Each brush-stroke was done with grace and care. But how could the picture be a clue to a violent and senseless murder?

Coroner Chen began to shake his head in disbelief. "Perhaps Fan-shing should have practised the old art-form throughout his life. He might have stood a better chance of earning a decent living for his wife and himself," he remarked, momentarily interrupting Judge Quan's chain of thought.

Face drawn and with deep lines showing, the Judge asked the Coroner to look for any hidden messages that Fan-shing might have placed somewhere on the painting.

Coroner Chen placed one hand on the edge of the painting and ran it lightly along the picture frame. There was nothing unusual. He then held the painting up against the window. The sun's light shone consistently through the fabric and there was nothing that he could find that was hidden within the painting. He placed it back on its stand, turned and walked dejectedly towards the Judge.

Coroner Chen was about to speak when Judge Quan raised his hands to stop him. The Judge gently stroked his short beard as he continued to look at the painting. Finally, Judge Quan also shook his head and with a deep sigh spoke softly in defeat. "This painting is our only link between Fan-shing and the murderer. There must be a clue within it and yet we are both unable to find or decipher a message of any sort." He rose to his feet and walked briskly the full length of the library, one hand still stroking his beard, contemplating the next move. Aware of the Judge's need for silence, Coroner Chen continued to look at the painting.

"We must act now, Coroner Chen," said Judge Quan. "You said you needed time off from the shop and to be with the people. I must now request you to do just that. Go to the various tea-houses in town. Be alert to see whether you can gather any clues about this case. A murderer who is able to cover all his tracks must be proud of his achievement and his tongue may slip under the influence of some wine. Go now, be careful; and report to me first thing tomorrow."

There was a tone of urgency in the Judge's voice. Coroner Chen knew that time was not on their side and so promptly took his leave.

Judge Quan felt that there was a chance that the perpetrator had already left town. But he hoped that the heightened tension within the town and his guards' close watch for anything unusual would deter the murderer from leaving. It would be premature to close the town's gates to prevent any escape. Such a measure would only bring more suffering to the people and to the town's commerce. No. They must act quickly to bring the case to an end.

Still considering various options, the Judge walked out of the library; his footsteps heavy on the wooden floor as he passed the Tribunal garden on his right. He crossed a small artificial bridge over the garden fish-pond and proceeded to the West Wing of the Tribunal where his living quarters were. He opened two large wooden doors and entered his bedroom. It was already lit by three candles and the Judge looked around, not knowing where an assistant had placed his clothes. He had rarely been in the room since his arrival in town; most nights had been spent in his comfortable library going through the town's documents. He moved towards his left and recognized a large wooden lacquered cabinet with five drawers at the front. He opened each drawer; progressively becoming more and more frustrated as he was unable to find what he was looking for ... until he opened the last drawer. Then the Judge smiled.

He took out a dark blue gown that he had worn at his Uncle's herbal shop. He could still smell the herbs as he quickly changed into the gown and felt the coolness of the fabric against his body. He tied his hair back but allowed a few strands to drop down against his face. Then he placed a round black cap on his head. Examining himself once more in the mirror, he felt satisfied that he no longer looked like a Magistrate.

He quickly – but silently – slipped out of the Tribunal's rear entrance and joined the busy evening scene in his town.

Not content with leaving Coroner Chen to do all the investigative work, Judge Quan felt a need to leave the comfortable confines of his library and Tribunal compound. He was determined to seek his own clues to this perplexing murder case.

Revenge from Beyond

Complainant Siu Begs Judge Quan for Justice .

Fan-Shing's Last Painting.

The Search for the Merchant's Body
Ends with a Discovery.

A Triumphant but Lonesome Judge Quan.

ii

CHAPTER SEVEN

*Unable to outrun his pursuer, the Judge had no choice but
eventually to stand and ward him off.
But to do so, he was determined to choose a place
where he stood a better chance of victory.*

Outside the Tribunal, Judge Quan slowed his pace to a leisurely walk. He turned a corner and saw an old man pushing a cart. Quite often large tea-house establishments would hire people to sell various types of noodles in the streets. Such sellers earned only meagre wages for their daily efforts, which explains why mainly elderly and poor people were employed.

Judge Quan approached the old man and offered several pieces of silver for a loan of his cart. He explained that he would return by the third watch of the night and that these pieces of silver were more then enough to compensate for the man's lost wages.

The old man looked at him suspiciously. This young man with torn and ragged clothes couldn't even afford half a piece of silver let alone the several pieces he had promised. But then his eyes opened wide and enthusiasm crept into his smile when the Judge took out a number of silver pieces from a wrapped white cloth. The old man thought that the younger man was insane, but at the same time he did not wish to miss out on a good opportunity. He eagerly offered the Judge his cart and, for his part, the Judge said that he would be back at the appointed time. Then he walked in the direction of the nearest gambling house.

The night was hot and humid, encouraging the townspeople to gather outdoors around the square. Where, during the daytime, there were shops and street stalls, a temporary stage had been erected and numerous amateur actors appeared, fully dressed in colourful and extravagant attire; their make-up and movements depicting heroes, warriors, commoners, and sometimes even gods and demons. A few of them revealed animated martial-art skills to the beat of drums and trumpets, played by a band situated behind the stage.

Bending his back slightly over the cart and moving at a constant but slow pace, the Judge proceeded towards the river, west of the Tribunal. The people out on the streets paid little or no attention to him. The Judge was happy that his disguise was working.

He continued to push the cart past the bridge and headed in the direction of Mrs Chu's house. He was now in the farming sector. Against the moonlit sky, the Judge could see people still tending their fields with the aid of lanterns. He could make out two men, working at a large wooden wheel. One side of the wheel scooped water and transferred it to a section on the other side of the wheel. This was how farmers irrigated their rice fields, an invention, thought the Judge, which simplified a farmer's tasks, ensuring a good harvest.

Before long, the Judge saw numerous lights coming from nearby houses and realized that Mrs Chu's house was nearby. He hid the noodle-cart amongst some scrub and continued by foot at a faster pace.

Guided by the moonlight overhead, Judge Quan was able to follow the route taken by the Tribunal earlier during his visit to Mrs Chu's residence. He followed the route by memory, skirting one avenue after another and avoiding brightly-lit places. It was some while before he stood in a dark alley-way between two long walls. He believed this to be the rear entrance to Mrs Chu's residence.

The Judge knelt in a crouching position and then jumped up and onto the top of the wall. Once on the top, he surveyed the wall and noticed that it ran along the rear and sides of each neighbouring house. Quietly he walked carefully along the wall until he stopped directly between Mrs Chu's and her neighbour's house and stood in silence, considering his next move.

The neighbour's first storey roof-line was a little higher than Judge Quan's height. This meant that he could move anywhere along the wall and observe Mrs Chu's house without being noticed. He was attempting to move closer for a better look when, suddenly he heard a door open. Mrs Chu walked into the yard. Still in her white mourning clothes, she held in her hands a pile of silver paper and some heavenly monetary notes. She walked to a burner and knelt before it, holding the pile of paper above her head for a long while. Then she lit the paper and cautiously placed the pile into the burner. She began to wail aloud as she watched the pile of paper burn to ash. Bowing several times, she stood up and walked back to her house, crying and thumping her chest in regret at the loss of her husband. As she re-entered the house, there was complete silence once more.

Judge Quan realized that Mrs Chu was adhering to the state law known as *Wufu*. The law states that there are five degrees of mourning-clothes that must be worn for a prescribed period during bereavement for a loved one. This evening, she wore the hemmed garments and straw shoes typical of the second degree for those who had lost their spouse. The first degree is reserved for those who have lost either one of their parents. The other three degrees were not as important and were usually not adhered to by the people and the Judiciary System.

As far as the Judge could see, Mrs Chu had burnt paper money that was sold in the town. The people believed that life still continues in one form or another in the world beyond. Similarly, the people believed that deceased persons have a need for money, clothes, food and houses in the after-life. Usually, paper miniatures of items such as these were burnt as offerings to the dead, symbolising the hope that the objects themselves would be transferred to the deceased.

Judge Quan's thoughts were distracted by loud whispering coming from Mrs Chu's kitchen. He quietly moved in closer to listen.

He recognized Mrs Chu's voice and, in the background, he could make out another voice, possibly that of a male. Unable to hear what was being said, he leaned closer and placed his ear against the kitchen wall. Suddenly he felt his feet sliding from the top of the roof. Unable to maintain his balance, he fell towards some wooden boxes placed next to the wall of the neighbour's house. The loud noise of broken wooden boxes disturbed the neighbour's chickens, and caused them to flap their wings and squawk loudly.

The Judge stood up shakily and realized that his right leg was bruised. He ran towards the rear wall, hurled himself over and landed in the dark alley-way once more. Racing away from the houses as fast as he could, he cursed himself for the clumsiness which could have jeopardized the whole investigation and revealed his true identity. Then, as he ran, he heard heavy footsteps closing in from behind him. He looked back and noticed that he was being chased. He tried to increase his pace, but the pain in his leg hindered his mobility. He swerved from one corner to the next, partly in an attempt to escape from his pursuer. But he had also lost his way in the dark and in the maze of tall walls and uninhabited streets.

Unable to outrun his pursuer, the Judge had no choice but to try to ward him off. He heard the man shouting from behind him. By this time, he had come to a clearing where there was ample room to move and fight. As the Judge prepared to make his stand, a man entered the same clearing and immediately stopped running. Both men stood face to face, breathless from the long pursuit.

"You swine! How dare you spy on someone else's home. What were you doing behind Mrs Chu's house?"

"What I do is none of your business. Stay away or you will regret what you have just said for the rest of your life." As he spoke, Judge Quan kept his eye on his opponent, satisfied that they were of similar build and that he would have an equal chance in a hand-to-hand combat.

The man came towards the Judge, positioning himself for an attack. The Judge moved to one side and parried the opponent's right-hand blow with his left. Then he held onto the attacker's hand and was about to strike a blow at the back of his opponent's head when the man regained his balance, struck the Judge's chest with a back-kick and sent him reeling towards the ground. The man then jumped into the air, aiming to land forcefully on Judge Quan. Using the ground as his support, Judge Quan raised his right leg and delivered a blow to his assailant's groin. The man landed next to the Judge, screaming in agony.

Judge Quan quickly stood up and moved away. The blow to his chest had made him lose his breath. He breathed deeply in and out several times, while keeping a close watch on his opponent.

The man stood up and began to move towards the Judge, his hands moving from his head to his face and then to his body, furiously stretching himself.

Realizing that his opponent was using the "monkey" style, Judge Quan stood sideways; apparently lost his balance and brought his right hand to his mouth, as if drinking a cup of wine. Then he moved his arms into the air and back down again as he drew nearer to his opponent.

The man saw that the Judge's "drunken" fighting style was limited and left his lower body exposed. As the two men closed in, the man threw himself to the ground once more, at the same time attempting to trip the Judge by a scissors action to both legs. Anticipating this move, the Judge quickly jumped into the air and tried to land down onto his opponent's chest. The man struck the Judge's legs with his own; and as both men's feet made contact, they used each other as support and kicked themselves away and clear from each other.

Both men stood at a distance face to face and now realized that they were equal.

"Well, not only is he a womanizer but he's not a bad fighter too! A person like you must attract and receive favours from many women. Was that why you were spying on Mrs Chu, hoping to subdue her with your strength? She may be a beautiful woman, but she's also a woman in mourning! Did that cross your dirty old mind?" The opponent was about to strike the Judge once more.

"Wait!" said the Judge. Although they were equal in hand-to-hand combat, he knew that his opponent was a well-trained seasoned fighter. Sooner or later he would succumb to the strength of his younger opponent.

"What were you doing there?" asked the Judge. "Perhaps you, too, wanted to gain the favour of Mrs Chu. As you just said, she is indeed a beautiful woman."

"Why you good-for-nothing dog's-head, I'll show you! Stand your ground!" The man once again ran towards the Judge.

Before the man could even come close to him, Judge Quan stood his ground and ripped his tunic apart to reveal the golden dragon insignia of a Magistrate of Sui-chou. The man stopped in his tracks, realizing that he had attacked the local Magistrate. He fell to his knees and bowed furiously to the Judge.

"Who are you? What were you doing near Mrs Chu's residence? Speak up now!" The Judge spoke in an authoritative voice. But, tired from the fight and dumbfounded, the kneeling man took some time to regain his breath and his thoughts.

"This person's name is E-Lung. I had just completed my evening meal with some friends and was walking back to my lodging. Since the night was still young and the air refreshing, I decided to take a different route back home. I was walking along a dark alley-way when I heard some commotion overhead and saw Your Honour climbing over Mrs Chu's wall and making your escape. My only thought was to capture you and report you to the authorities. Little did I realize that it was you, the Magistrate himself." E-Lung bowed his head; resigning his fate to the Judge who stood before him.

"For a commoner, your martial arts are indeed exceptional. Who taught you to fight and what do you do for a living?" asked the Judge, curious.

"My late father trained my blood brother and myself in the arts of self-defense. We both served in the Emperor's military for more then six years. In a campaign against the Mongol hordes up North, the General used the left flank of the army as a decoy and then struck the Mongols with his right flank. The left flank stood no chance and in the ensuing battle, I lost my brother. I was so incensed by the General's methods, I decided to desert and left the military of my own accord. I have travelled to many places; but recently I settled in this town while deciding my next move."

The Judge examined E-lung's face; it showed a man full of anger at the senseless loss of his brother. But to desert from the military ultimately meant capital punishment. Obviously, E-lung travelled from town to town, living in fear of being arrested by the authorities, unable to settle permanently as he had not been officially discharged from the military. In the eyes of the law, E-Lung was a criminal, no better than any murderer.

"E-Lung," Judge Quan pronounced, after some moments of careful thought. "You are now under arrest for hindering an official murder investigation by the Tribunal and for unlawful desertion from the Empire's military without an official discharge. You will be taken to the Tribunal and your case will be heard by me in court; three days later, if approval is received from the Prefecture, you will be sentenced to death for your betrayal of the Empire."

E-Lung realized that his time had come. For many years he had been on the run, dreading this moment. He had always known that he could hide or use self-defence to protect himself from the authorities but that, one day, he would be overpowered by someone more cunning and able then he was. He knew that it was his time right now. Resigned to his fate, he lowered his head to the Judge in silence.

Judge Quan was impressed with this man's speed, strength and agility. He must have had a life-long training in fighting since he had anticipated the Judge's every move. Such a man and his skills should not be wasted.

"Considering that you have suffered from the loss of your brother and have lived a lonely and secluded life for many years, I sentence you now to assist me as my constable during the investigation of this murder case. For your efforts, I will provide a recommendation for your official discharge from the military. Of course, it will not be an honourable discharge, but it will mean that you are a free person. But only if you apply your skills to my murder investigation," the Judge concluded with a smile.

E-Lung bowed his head and thanked the Judge profusely. He promised to serve the Judge diligently during the course of this investigation, and beyond. Judge Quan smiled and took E-Lung's hands and raised him to his feet. He patted E-Lung's back and told him that he could stay at the Tribunal compound until he found a favourable lodging.

Back at the Tribunal, Judge Quan left E-Lung and instructed an assistant to take him to his new lodgings within the Tribunal compound. Judge Quan himself settled back in his library and wrote a letter of pardon for E-Lung from the military. He then handed the letter to a Tribunal courier who would promptly deliver the letter to the Prefect by horse.

Satisfied that E-Lung was now free, Judge Quan leaned back in this seat and stared at Fan-shing's painting. His eyes were on the painting, but his thoughts were on Coroner Chen. The Judge thought that he might have been hasty in assigning such a difficult and dangerous task to the herbalist and wondered if he had had any success in his enquiries.

CHAPTER EIGHT

As an individual clings to his or her loved ones and possessions
during life, so too will some cling on
if life is suddenly taken away from them.

Early next morning, Judge Quan, Coroner Chen and the new recruit, E-Lung, gathered at the Tribunal library.

"Coroner Chen, I would like you to meet our new constable, E-Lung".

Judge Quan gave a brief account of how he had met E-Lung the previous night. Both Coroner Chen and E-Lung then bowed to each other as a show of respect between two new Tribunal colleagues.

Judge Quan thanked each of his new assistants for accepting his offer of a service to the Tribunal. He stressed to both that the tasks before them were difficult, but not impossible to resolve. He wanted them to take great care and to be diligent while the murderer was still at large. The Judge made it clear that all three of them were new and inexperienced in their roles. That made the whole investigation much more dangerous and challenging.

"Coroner Chen, you said you had some important developments to report?" Judge Quan sat back in his chair and began to listen attentively to Coroner Chen. E-Lung remained standing next to the Judge.

"Well, I went to several tea-houses as Your Honour instructed. As you thought might be the case, news about Fan-shing's death was the main topic of the night. The circumstances of the murder were told and re-told, with several variations.

"I was taking my evening meal in one of the tea-houses when a young man, probably in his late twenties, decided to sit at my table, despite not being invited. He started to complain about how demanding and arrogant the Guild-Master of the Hotel Sheng Lu-ching was to his staff.

"Since he was an employee of Lu-ching's hotel, I thought he might be able to comment on some of the rumours that were being circulated. I invited him to join me in my meal and ordered some wine for my new companion. As the wine flowed, so did the conversation. Soon it led to the subject of Candidate Soong.

"He said that Candidate Soong was never an intelligent and dedicated student. He was a womanizer and not a scholar. He appeared outwardly intelligent only because he constantly lived in his father's shadow. He aspired to his father's reputation, but did not have the same shrewdness as his father. With his various family connections, Candidate Soong apparently arranged to have his Judiciary Examination marked in such a way that he would pass the tests with top marks."

"But how could one falsify a Judiciary examination? I thought arrangements were made to eliminate such a possibility?" E-Lung queried.

Judge Quan explained that a Candidate could buy the favour of one of the examiners. The answer-papers did not bear the names of each Candidate. The only way to identify a Candidate from his answer-paper was by a number written on the top of each answer-sheet and this number was allocated only at the point of entry to the examination-hall.

"So there was no way for an examiner to know which candidate's examination-paper he was marking?" said E-Lung.

"Correct! But all answers must be written in poetic phrases. Therefore, an examiner could still identify a paper's owner by the opening phrase used in the first or second answer."

"But there must be over five hundred Candidates per examination and up to ten examiners; how could one ensure that a particular examiner would mark a particular Candidate's answer-paper?" said E-Lung, continuing to reveal his judiciary inexperience.

"With Candidate Soong's name and connections, it comes as no surprise that some examiners may have been bribed. If an examiner did not co-operate, he would be blacklisted, never again to see another examination paper.

"The Judiciary examination system is the only means by which to select talented Candidates able to govern and lead the people of this vast land. It has therefore important implications for the Empire since the correct people must be selected fairly.

"Since people from all walks of life have an equal opportunity to sit for an examination, safeguards have been introduced to ensure that only the most talented are selected. But, as long as there are corrupt officials, there will always be ways to circumvent these safeguards." Judge Quan concluded his explanation to both his men and then stood up and ordered the Coroner to ask the Tribunal archivist to bring the preliminary local examination results to the library.

As the Coroner left the room, E-Lung was left alone with Judge Quan. He observed the Judge's impatience as he paced back and forth along the length of the library, both arms behind his back. When the Coroner re-entered with the archivist, each man carried a scroll. The scrolls were presented to the Judge with both hands and after the Judge had accepted them, he dismissed the archivist with a few kind words.

Judge Quan and the Coroner examined their own scrolls at length. At times, they interchanged each other's scrolls before the Judge looked up, caressed his beard and spoke.

"It appears that the Candidate received only average marks in the preliminary examination. So much so, he only just made it through to the actual examination. Yet it was in this examination that he came first. Either he was a brilliant student who spent night and day after the preliminary examination on his studies, or he received help from others."

Coroner Chen continued to study the scroll. After a short time his face contorted apparently in anger as he mumbled to himself, "Curious how Tax-Collector Tang bai-tu also sat for the final exam!"

"Tax Collector who?" Somewhat annoyed, the Judge interrupted the Coroner's musings.

Coroner Chen shook his head quickly and looked at the Judge. "Your Honour's predecessor presided over the final examination as is customary in all local examinations, and there were eight examiners marking all the Candidates' papers in this instance. It appears quite convenient that all the examiners and your predecessor have left this town, all but one, so called Examiner Shao." Coroner Chen looked at the Judge.

"What else did your table companion say?" Judge Quan asked. "Did he make any comment as to how Candidate Soong's examination marks connect him with our murder case?"

"According to him, Candidate Soong first met Mrs Chu one day at Fan-shing's gallery, but it wasn't until Candidate Soong attended a dance performance by Mrs Chu at the hotel that the two appeared to strike up a relationship. From then onwards, at each subsequent performance by Mrs Chu, she and Candidate

Soong appeared inseparable, at least according to my table guest."

"Perhaps, your table companion was right," said the Judge. "Candidate Soong's close relationship to Mrs Chu meant that her husband was in their way and this may have led to the plot against Fan-shing. It may also explain Candidate Soong's nervous appearace at my welcome dinner banquet. The Candidate's close scrutiny of the Tribunal procession to Mrs Chu's residence yesterday also serves to reinforce the suspicion of his involvement in the murder case.

"Unfortunately, this is not hard evidence which we can use in court. We must find definite evidence to link candidate Soong to the murder and that in turn should link Mrs Chu to her husband's demise.

"But how does Fang-shing's painting connect to the murder case?" Judge Quan slumped back on his seat and continued to reflect on the case and their progress with it.

For the first time, E-Lung approached the painting, for a closer look.

"We now have a murderer at large and an accomplice. To their dissatisfaction, the people of this town will learn today that the Tribunal has gathered little evidence to resolve this murder case. We must double our efforts in order to gather more clues and we must do it quickly."

"Your Honour!" E-Lung interrupted the Judge. "I've seen this bridge before. Well, at least one that looks like it."

"Where?" The Judge turned around and faced E-Lung like a tiger about to pounce on his prey. "Where? Where did you see this bridge?"

"In the mountainous regions, west of this town. The mountains are an ideal place for me to practice my archery skills, and the animals I manage to kill can often be sold at the market for a handsome price. I've seen a bridge similar to the one in this painting, except there was no pavilion and definitely no such views as depicted in the painting," E-Lung answered proudly. For the first time he felt that he was contributing to the case.

"Did you ever cross the bridge?" Judge Quan enquired.

"No, Your Honour. I was told by travelling merchants that an old hermit used the bridge and strange stories were told of how people had gone missing, once they'd crossed. Those who managed to return reported losing trace of time and indeed, after only a few days absence, returned looking many years older. I liked the way I looked, thanks; and all I wanted was to have a good day's hunting and go back to town for a few glasses of fine wine and a nice wench to be with."

E-Lung concluded as Judge Quan smiled at him. It never failed to amaze the Judge how military personnel's lives always revolved around females and wine.

"That must be the old hermit, Lao Tzu," Coroner Chen interrupted. "His hair and beard are so long and white that some people think that he looks like the Great Sage, founder of Taoism. As to the rumours, well no-one has really crossed the bridge because the rumours alone are enough to scare them."

Judge Quan leaned back in his seat and for a good while stared into empty space as if in a state of trance. Coroner Chen began to pour the Judge a cup of hot tea, but was suddenly startled when the Judge slammed his hands, stood up and walked over to the painting. Speaking loudly and enthusiastically, the Judge continued. "The perplexing problems surrounding this murder case have clouded my memory. Yesterday morning I had a dream, I was invited to cross over an old wooden bridge by a beautiful long-haired woman. As I began to walk onto the wooden planks, it fell to pieces beneath me and soon I found myself falling into the darkness beneath."

Judge Quan detected curious looks from his assistants.

"Can't you see? The bridge in my dream and this painting, the long haired woman and Mrs Chu? This explains why I was so much attracted to this painting in the first instance. I questioned that strange attraction initially at Mrs Chu's residence, but never gave it another moment's thought. The fall I experienced in my dream indicates that grave danger lies ahead of us."

Judge Quan looked at his assistants once more and saw that they were sceptical. He smiled and proceeded to explain himself. "A Judge always goes by hard facts, but intuition also plays a major role in any investigation, especially where an investigation has no real leads, as in our case. Intuition comes at any moment, maybe in the form of a thought or dream. I, for one, cannot explain to you about the after-life and ghosts, but as an individual clings to his or her loved ones and possessions during life, so too will some cling on if life is suddenly taken away from them. Those who cling on like this feel that they have unfinished work; some stay and use whatever means are needed to complete their tasks. Perhaps Fan Shing approached me in the form of a dream and gave me some clues. The closeness between the dream and the murder case is beyond any doubt. We must pay this bridge and the old hermit a visit. As for Mrs Chu, we must all be careful. She is not the woman she portrays and wants us to believe. I am convinced that she was directly involved in the demise of Fan-shing. Why and how, only time will tell, and it is time that may catch up with Mrs Chu herself.

"E-Lung!" Judge Quan ordered, "After the morning session, I want you to take me to see that bridge, while Coroner Chen must track down Examiner Shao and see whether he played a part in Candidate Soong's successful – though dubious – examination result. You may then return to the crime scene; find out what you can and how the poison was applied without it affecting Mrs Chu. But more importantly look for any trace of a male who was present with Mrs Chu last night. We must act and act fast before the people become angered with the Tribunal's lack of progress."

After the Judge finished speaking to his assistants, the Tribunal bells sounded outside. The Judge was quickly helped into his Magistrate's clothes by E-Lung, while Coroner Chen refilled a teacup and offered it to the Judge.

As the Judge proceeded to the court, his two new assistants followed behind him. Both were excited about their appointments to the Tribunal's services, but at the same time they were nervous about what might lie ahead.

CHAPTER NINE

A person must be deeply asleep or previously dead
not to wake up and struggle
against a fire consuming him.

Judge Quan stood behind the courtroom bench and surveyed the scene before him. All the Tribunal guards were standing to attention. Behind them were the public attendees. Amongst the crowd was Mrs Chu, wearing her usual white mourning clothes and her long and sensuous hair.

After he had rapped once with the gavel, the Judge pronounced that the morning court session was open.

"I, Magistrate of Sui-chou, have been responsible for this jurisdiction for the past six days and until now, I have not appointed any assistants to aid me in my work. In the light of the Fan-shing murder case, however, my responsibilities have increased manifold. I am therefore delighted to announce the appointment of two able men who will assist me in my daily tasks."

Judge Quan asked Coroner Chen and E-Lung to stand in front of the bench. Indicating that the Coroner should stand in the position behind him on the left, the place usually reserved for the second ranking Tribunal officer, the Judge announced that, from that day onwards, Coroner Chen would serve as Sergeant. He would assist and advise the Judge on all court matters.

Then the Judge announced that E-Lung was appointed Constable. He would oversee all operational tasks within the Tribunal and be Captain of the entire contingent of Tribunal officers. E-Lung was invited to stand on the Judge's right, the place reserved for the third ranking Tribunal officer.

"Let it be known that now that the court has the assistance of these two able men, the Fan-shing murder case will progress faster from here onwards. The Tribunal wishes to convey its condolences to Mrs Chu and I am sure she will want this case to be resolved quickly in order that she can provide a proper and decent burial for her husband."

Mrs Chu smiled quietly to herself. From the Judge's comment she knew that he had not found the identity of the murderer and that no solid evidence had been found to progress the case any further. She bowed low to the Judge in acceptance of his sympathy and then asked him for permission to approach the bench. Judge Quan reluctantly acknowledged her.

As she moved slowly and gracefully to the bench and bowed to the Judge, she was aware that everyone was watching her. She spoke softly and clearly for all to hear. "As the court knows, I am still mourning the loss of my beloved husband." At this point she began to weep but made an attempt to hold back her tears. "I express my gratitude towards the court for their words of concern towards me. However, it has been more then a day since the discovery of my husband's murder and my husband's spirit has not yet been appeased."

Judge Quan had known Mrs Chu would express her concerns about the slow progress being made in solving her husband's murder. In expressing these concerns, she criticised the court's slow process openly but in a subtle way, short of being in contempt of the Tribunal.

"Despite my grief, I have instigated a thorough search of my husband's belongings and have found to my horror that two of his paintings have been stolen." Mrs Chu emphasised the last sentence of her speech for all to hear.

Noise filled the courtroom for some time as Judge Quan continued to stare at Mrs Chu, disturbed that a person in the midst of her grief had managed to uncover a crucial piece of evidence.

"How did you discover that there were two paintings missing and since when have you known this?" The Judge questioned, while at the same time rapping the gavel against the Tribunal desk. Mrs Chu did not answer until order was restored in the court.

"At first, it did not occur to me. While Your Honour was directing his attention to calming my grief, I realized that my husband's inventory of artworks had not been checked. It appeared that the investigation was focusing on me and on our bedroom."

Once again the courtroom was in an uproar. All those present appeared to be on the side of Mrs Chu. They sympathized with a wife who had had to make the supreme effort to delve into her husband's belongings in the midst of her greatest loss. On the other hand, the Tribunal had done little to resolve the case and had made no effort to protect the common people.

Judge Quan stood up and slammed his hands so hard against the desk that one of the placards marked "death by hanging" fell onto the floor. Everyone fell silent in the courtroom. He was furious at the subtle ways in which Mrs Chu had accused him of directing his favours onto her, and because she had also indirectly indicated the Tribunal's incompetence in carrying out an incomplete search of the crime scene.

The Judge saw the placard and realized that it was facing directly at him. He immediately sat down in silence.

Coroner Chen worried that the longer Mrs Chu was allowed to speak, the more slanders she would bring against the Judge. Until now, Judge Quan had shown great patience and competence. But he was not sure whether the Judge's lack of experience would enable him to withstand Mrs Chu's cunning and vindictive personal attack.

The Judge slumped in his chair and wondered how he could have missed such an important clue to the murder. Indeed, he should have conducted a more thorough search of the residence. Then perhaps he would have been able to uncover the missing artworks, thus throwing new light on the case.

Keeping his voice low and soft as if dejected, he proceeded to announce as follows: "This Tribunal would again like to express its gratitude to Mrs Chu for her diligent work. From here onwards, the Tribunal will proceed with speed and settle once and for all who stole Fan-shing's paintings."

Then Judge Quan immediately rapped with the gavel to adjourn the court session. He stood up and was about to leave when a cry was heard from outside the courtroom.

"Your Honour! Fire! My hotel! Fire!" The oversized Hotel Guild-Master waddled his way towards the bench and pushed the guard aside as he clumsily knelt and bowed to the Judge.

"Your Honour, my hotel..."

Judge Quan angrily cut short the Guild-Master's speech. "Hold your tongue, or the court will reward you with thirty lashes for your lapse of memory."

The Hotel Guild master ceased to speak but continued to breathe heavily. Judge Quan returned to his seat and asked the Guild-Master to state his name for the Tribunal record.

"Your Honour, this insignificant person is Sheng Lu-ching, Hotel Guild-Master of this town. As you know, I operate a hotel next to the river. In the middle of the night, I was awakened by a strong smell of burning wood and my assistant rushed into my room and reported that one of the wings of my hotel was on fire." The Guild-Master paused to catch his breath.

Judge Quan was annoyed that more work would have to be done which would take him away from solving the Fan-shing murder case. He impatiently gestured to the Guild-Master to continue.

"We were prepared for this situation and have put the required measures in place, so we managed to put the fire out quickly. But judging from the degree of damage, I am afraid the fire was intense before we could get to it. When the fire was out, my assistant did a quick preliminary check of the damage, and to his great surprise, he discovered a burnt body in one of the rooms. I was so aghast that I immediately came here to report this unfortunate incident. I beg Your Honour to find out the cause of the fire. I cannot sleep from knowing that a person died in my own hotel, I...."

"Has everyone else been accounted for?" Judge Quan quickly interrupted, annoyed that the Guild-Master had already finished his report and had taken the time to press the Tribunal to launch a prompt investigation so that he could return his hotel back to full business capacity for his own gain.

"I am afraid that I have had little time to do so. Immediately after the body was found, I came to the Tribunal to make a report. My assistant was still continuing the count when I left, Your Honour."

"And yet you still had time to evaluate the damage before you came to report the fire? I think that if no human remains had been found, you might perhaps have taken your time to report to the Tribunal. Alas, since one of your guests has died, you felt that a bad omen had befallen your business and only then did you rush to this court for help. Let me tell you and the court, that this Tribunal will always launch prompt and thorough investigations, irrespective of who has reported a case. The court acknowledges no difference between the well-off and the poor. They all have an equal opportunity in the court. Do you understand?"

The Hotel Guild-Master answered in the affirmative and wondered what he had done to deserve such a strong reprimand from the Judge. Judge Quan announced that he would immediately investigate the scene of the fire and ordered a guard to prepare his palanquin. He quickly adjourned the morning court session and stormed out of the courtroom into his library.

Coroner Chen and E-Lung followed the Judge to his library. Judge Quan's face was flushed with anger at Mrs Chu's personal accusation. For the first time, the Judge realized that she was not going to be easy to deal with.

Judge Quan leaned out of the Tribunal window and looked out on the still scenery of this private garden. The hotel fire would certainly take him away from any immediate investigations relating to the Fan-shing case. He must delay his trip to the mountain with E-Lung and direct his efforts at the hotel, while Coroner Chen must speak to Examiner Shao, and make another inspection at Mrs Chu's residence as planned.

"Your Honour, the palanquin is ready for you!" E-Lung interrupted Judge Quan's thoughts. The Judge turned around to face the Coroner.

"Go to Examiner Shao and find out what you can about Candidate Soong. Then proceed to Mrs Chu's residence and find out what paintings are missing. Look for clues as to how the poison was applied. Go immediately! There is no time to waste." The Judge then turned to E-Lung and signalled that they both must leave now for the hotel.

A large number of people had already gathered outside the hotel, awaiting the Judge's arrival. Everyone was amazed at the extent of the damage.

Judge Quan entered the hotel and saw for himself that the top floor was almost entirely destroyed. He could still feel the heat emanating from the charred remains from above. It appeared that no-one could have survived.

"There were only ten rooms in this wing. I had plans to extend the wing; but the way it is, that may be premature." The Hotel Guild-Master looked down dejectedly.

"Was anyone else caught in the fire? Were any possessions recovered intact?"

"Upon my return from the Tribunal, I checked with my assistant. Fortunately, there weren't many guests staying in this

64

part of the hotel. Most of them were out in the tea-house late into the night, drinking and gambling," the Guild-Master answered.

"All guests except for one. Where is the victim?"

"On the upper floor. The Warden is outside the room, guarding it until Your Honour's arrival." The Guild-Master pointed to where a young man stood upstairs.

Judge Quan quickly walked up the staircase and realized that yet another person had died in his jurisdiction within two days. Surely, his wish for a challenging case had been answered two-fold! But he could not help but feel that bad omens had befallen this town.

He noticed that part of the charred staircase had collapsed but he could see that it had been hastily repaired in time for his inspection. Apparently, the Guild-Master believed in preserving his investments and in doing so had taken adequate steps to prevent or minimize damage. His detailed work and quick thinking were the reason why he had been continuously elected as the town's Hotel Guild-Master.

The Warden bowed low as the Judge and E-Lung approached the room. Judge Quan asked him whether anything had been tampered with, to which he replied that he had arrived when the fire was still burning and had helped to put the fire out. He immediately sealed off and guarded the room personally after the victim was discovered in the room. No one had entered the room since.

Judge Quan congratulated the Warden for a job well done and asked him to instruct one of the Tribunal's guards to replace him. The Warden was to return home for a well earned rest.

Judge Quan and E-Lung entered the heavily polluted room. The walls had been eaten away by the fire and a portion of the roof had collapsed, allowing a beam of sunlight to shine in. With this as the only source of light, the charred remains of a person still seated and slumped over a table could just be seen in the middle of the room.

The Judge instructed E-Lung to search and inspect what remained of the room, while he began an examination of the body. Much of the clothing had been burned, but from what little remained of the body the Judge noted that it was a male. The skin was dry and wrinkled by the flames and only traces of hair remained. The face, too, was beyond recognition, as both the eyelids had been sealed by the intense flames.

Slowly the Judge moved himself around the body. He was perplexed as to how the candle-holder and two other chairs nearby were still left standing and undisturbed, and he felt that the victim would surely have struggled against the flames. But there were few signs to suggest that that was what had happened.

E-Lung ignored the silence and reported that the fire must have started at the tea-stove since apparently the water was left boiling and unattended. Perhaps the boiling water spilled over the hot coals and caught fire, eventually engulfing the whole room and the hotel wing.

The Judge nodded and instructed E-Lung to go and fetch the Guild-Master. After E-Lung had departed, Judge Quan picked up a burned stick and used it slowly to pry open the victim's mouth. The intensity of the heat had almost sealed the lips, but with a little effort the Judge managed to open the mouth slightly. He tried to look inside but was unable to do so, due to the limited light in the room.

E-Lung and the Guild-Master now entered the room. Judge Quan immediately stopped his examination and turned to face the Guild-Master.

"Do you know the name of the victim?"

"Our record shows that he was a rice merchant by the name of He. He was in town on business and checked in two days ago."

As he put a lighted candle on the table, E-Lung asked, "Did he leave any possessions in the care of the hotel? I can't find any trace of his belongings." The Guild-Master answered that all patrons' belongings were locked securely in a safe in the hotel office. He would go to find out whether the victim had previously left his possessions in the safe.

When the Guild-Master left the room, Judge Quan quickly took the lighted candle and placed it near the victim's face. He resumed his examination while E-Lung moved in for a closer look. When the Judge opened the mouth, this time he could see inside clearly. The victim's teeth were still intact while the tongue and the walls of the mouth were dry. There were no traces of charring and the inner cheeks were flesh red in color.

The Judge stood back, stroking his beard with his right hand, deep in thought as he walked to the tea-stove. E-Lung immediately took the stick and once more examined the victim's mouth, not knowing what had caught the Judge's attention.

"You're right E-Lung," the Judge began to speak. "The fire did indeed start at the stove. But why was it left unattended? Furthermore, the victim showed no signs of a struggle, as is apparent from the candle-holder and chairs that are still left standing.

"That would not be too unusual, Your Honour." E-Lung looked up at the Judge as he said this and stopped his examination. "Most merchants like to drink as part of their business dealings with potential customers. This might mean that the victim was drunk. Unable to walk over to his bed, he slumped over the table in the middle of the room and slept before the fire began."

"Maybe so; a person must be deeply asleep or previously dead not to wake up and struggle against a fire consuming him," the Judge replied.

E-Lung raised his eyebrow, amazed that the Judge had already concluded the victim was dead before the fire, but how was he to prove this?

Judge Quan sensed E-Lung's bewilderment; he smiled and replied that Coroner Chen would be the only person to prove that point. At that moment, the Guild-Master entered the room carrying a large bag in his hand.

"This bag was the only possession left in the care of the hotel by Merchant He, Your Honour." He handed the bag to the Judge who immediately searched it. There was nothing of relevance in the bag, just some silver money and travel and business documents wrapped in a scroll by a thin cord. As the Judge and E-Lung unscrolled a business document each, they were surprised to find they were not documents, but paintings. By the look of the brush-strokes, Judge Quan recognized they had been done by Fan-shing. He looked up at E-Lung, bewildered, and then looked back down at the charred body remains of Merchant He.

The Judge spoke softly. "These are the paintings reported stolen from Fan-shing's gallery."

CHAPTER TEN

*I am still the Magistrate of Sui-chou. I am the representative of
the August Moon Emperor of this great land.
How dare you treat the Emperor's law with contempt?*

This new twist in the Fan-shing murder case was later conveyed to Coroner Chen as all three men gathered around Judge Quan's library table. Coroner Chen was surprised that Merchant He had had in his possession the two reported missing paintings.

"Could it be that the Rice-merchant killed Fan-shing because of some grudge, gained entry to the Chu residence, saw and stole the paintings?" E-Lung asked.

"Yes, but how did Merchant He die? According to Your Honour, the Rice-merchant put up little or no struggle against the flames? Who would want to kill the Rice-merchant and what relation does this person have with Fan-shing?" the Coroner asked.

"We know that merchants have a habit of gambling and we also know that Fan-shing loved to gamble. Perhaps Fan-shing owed a considerable amount of money to Merchant He, which could explain why Fan-shing painted his last work. He was unable to finish it and so Merchant He, angered by the large sum of money owed to him, hired a thief to burgle and at the same time kill Fan-shing. It was a cruel act, but it may have appeased the Merchant's anger and he may have thought that the stolen paintings would fetch a handsome price to cover his loss." The Judge had given a plausible answer to Coroner Chen's questions, but he also knew that his explanations had several fatal flaws.

"As to the lack of evident struggle by Merchant He, you, my friend, will be the person to answer some of those questions for us," said the Judge to Coroner Chen. "Unfortunately, through lack of evidence, we can only propose explanations to our questions. We must seek that evidence before making any definite judgement. Did you manage to track down Examiner Shao and did you find anything else at Mrs Chu's residence?"

Judge Quan sat back on his chair and, with folded arms, listened to Coroner Chen's report of his investigation.

"After Your Honour's departure to the hotel, I examined the Tribunal records and found that Examiner Shao lived in the north-eastern – more affluent – part of this town. When I proceeded there, a man greeted me, probably in his seventies. When I asked for Examiner Shao, he replied that he was that person. I noticed many of his front teeth were missing, but apart from that his voice and speech were remarkably clear for a man of his age.

When I introduced myself as the Sergeant of the Tribunal, I could see that he was disturbed. I tried to assure him that I only wanted to ask some questions about Candidate Soong, but his face turned red and he immediately slammed the door. I heard footsteps walking away. As Examiner Shao was not directly implicated in the murder case, I decided not to pursue him further, but to ask Your Honour what our next move should be." Coroner Chen paused for the Judge to speak.

"It is imperative that we should question him about Candidate Soong. If Candidate Soong indeed bribed his way through the examination, his title must be revoked. It would be inappropriate to summon Examiner Shao to court. I will send my visiting card and try to see him personally."

The Judge quickly wrote some words on a red visiting card and imprinted it with the Tribunal seal. He then passed this card to E-Lung who would later order a messenger to deliver it to the Examiner.

Then Coroner Chen continued with his report. "I immediately proceeded back to the Tribunal prior to visiting Mrs Chu's residence. I thought Mrs Chu might give us trouble because of another intrusion, so I decided to ask two Tribunal guards to accompany me.

As expected, Mrs Chu was reluctant to let us in, as she apparently wanted no visitors during the period of her mourning. I told her that I was no visitor but was here in relation to the Tribunal investigation. I pointed to the two guards and indicated to her strongly that they were there to ensure that my task was completed. Only then did she let us in.

"Inside the reception gallery, I saw Fan-shing's body lying on a make-shift table. The dark blue spots on his face were still evident. Mrs Chu continued her loud crying and burned more paper money on her husband's behalf. Next to her was a

Buddhist monk, chanting sutras to ease Fan-shing's safe passage to the other world. While Mrs Chu continued with the duties of her bereavement, I proceeded up to the bedroom, posting one of the guards at the staircase and the other outside the room.

"To cut a long story short, I found nothing out of the usual in the room, but I can confidently say that I now know the way the poison was administered to Fan-shing."

"How?" asked the Judge, sitting up straight in his chair and looking excitedly at the Coroner.

"I carefully examined the walls of the bedroom where the bed stood, remembering that Fan-shing died with his face towards the wall. I spotted a small hole in the wooden wall, no smaller then the smallest bamboo musical pipe. It takes only a small speck of the poison to kill and a small pipe could have been used to administer the poison. All the killer had to do was to stand outside, on the neighbour's roof almost exactly where Your Honour stood last night. We know the shadows from the two houses meant that the murderer could not be detected. The pipe with the poison was inserted through a small hole in the wall and placed close to Fan-shing's face. A small and quiet blow into the pipe would have effectively administered the poison and no trace of the substance would remain. It was quiet, clean and effective."

"Why then were we unable to notice that hole in the first place?" the Judge asked.

"We couldn't! I only noticed it from outside the house. Some filling covered the hole from within the room, and the bed was placed right against the wall, blocking the site of the hole from full view. The murderer had only to apply the poison and block the hole. Then all that Mrs Chu had to do was push the bed against the wall to hide the evidence."

"Well done, brother!" An elated E-Lung shouted. "Now we know how the murder took place."

Judge Quan stood up from his chair and faced his assistants. He, too, was elated but agreed with them that they still did not know the motives behind the murder and had no real substantial evidence that would link both Mrs Chu and Candidate Soong to each other and to the crime. The Judge gave a deep sigh. They now had two murder cases, each linked to the other by Fan-shing's paintings. Both were cunningly executed, but for what reasons?

Judge Quan looked at Fan-shing's painting, while he continued to share his thoughts. At the afternoon session, Mrs Chu would want answers as to why the Tribunal had conducted a second investigation at her place. Heaven knows what sort of accusations she would contrive against the court, but the Judge's greatest fear was the people. They would be more apprehensive now that two murder cases had surfaced. They would rightly fear for their safety. All this talk and rumour served only to frighten people and business away from the town. The Capital would start to ask questions and the Tribunal had no answers.

Then the Tribunal drums sounded for the start of the afternoon session. Coroner Chen helped the Judge into his ceremonial clothes without a word spoken. As Judge Quan walked towards the courtroom, E-Lung and the Coroner followed behind.

By now the courtroom was packed with an agitated crowd. All had heard about the burnt rice merchant found dead at the hotel. As Judge Quan entered the courtroom with his assistants, the whole court became silent. The Judge surveyed the crowd and noticed Mrs Chu, still clad in white. Not too far from her stood Candidate Soong. The Judge sat down and proceeded to open the afternoon session.

He looked at Mrs Chu. Her face was drawn and solemn. She wept intermittently and an elderly woman next to her tried to comfort her. Candidate Soong looked at the Judge intently. All along he avoided gazing at Mrs Chu. Judge Quan wondered why the Candidate, surely implicated in Fan-shing's murder, had suddenly decided to make his presence known in court.

As the Judge was about to announce to the Tribunal his conclusions on how Fan-shing was killed, Mrs Chu stepped forward once more, knelt in front of the Judge; prostrated herself and complained that she had been mistreated. A guard nearby was about to step forward and reprimand her for speaking out of turn, but Judge Quan raised his hand to stop him.

"Speak up and make your point quickly!" the Judge snapped at Mrs Chu. With tears still in her eyes she looked up to face the Judge.

"As the court knows, I am in a state of mourning for the loss of my beloved husband. But this morning Your Honour sent some men to my home, who claimed to be investigating my husband's murder, intimidating me with two fully armed Tribunal guards. All this happened in the presence of a venerable priest who was presiding over prayers and chanting for the sake of my husband's soul. I cannot but worry that my husband's spirit may never be laid to rest when his widowed wife is constantly hounded by the Tribunal and unable to finish her dutiful tasks of giving her husband a proper burial." She began to weep once more.

"It is part of our ongoing investigation. You, Mrs Chu, earlier accused the court of complacency. Now that the court is taking prompt action, you accuse it of disturbing your peace. As far as this Tribunal is concerned, your husband will be at peace when his murderer is brought to trial.

"If Mrs Chu feels that the Tribunal was intimidating her by the launch of a second investigation at her residence today, then let it be known that, through that investigation, this court has found out how Fan-shing was murdered."

The courtroom's silence was immediately broken by many voicing their surprise at the announcement of this new development, while some in the crowd attempted to quieten their neighbours and listen to what the Judge had to say next.

"Fan-shing was killed by poison blown from a bamboo pipe inserted through a hole in the bedroom wall next to his bed," the Judge announced.

When they had absorbed this statement, visitors in the courtroom were appalled at the sinister act now revealed to them.

Judge Quan gazed at Mrs Chu and Candidate Soong in turn. Mrs Chu immediately wept even louder. She stood up and then fell back immediately onto the floor, while Candidate Soong remained passive.

Judge Quan ordered a guard to treat Mrs Chu. The guard promptly brought sour tea for her to drink, after which she slowly regained her consciousness. Judge Quan sat back in his seat, his right hand caressing his beard, observing Mrs Chu's theatrics whilst also focusing on Candidate Soong.

There were still murmurs in the courtroom when the Judge continued. "This Tribunal has also found the two paintings that Mrs Chu reported as missing during this morning's session."

Mrs Chu looked up at the Judge, her eyes growing wider and the courtroom silence was again broken.

"The fire-victim found at the hotel this morning was in possession of Fan-shing's lost paintings," the Judge announced.

Mrs Chu's sad and tearful mood immediately changed. She began bowing to the Judge profusely, thanking him for the resolution of her husband's murder. She stood up and paced happily around the court screaming cries of joy now that her husband could be buried with dignity. Judge Quan once again looked at this delirious woman, not comprehending one single word she said. Once again, determined to be the centre of attraction, she had succeeded in turning attention back to her. Her ostentatious theatrical displays had turned this courtroom into her stage, performing an art she knew so well.

"Guard! Hold that woman and don't let go of her before she is given twenty lashes!" Judge Quan ordered. Two guards swiftly grabbed Mrs Chu by her hands and one jabbed her with his fist, which forced her to kneel down onto the floor. As she landed heavily against the hard ground, she let out a loud cry. The two guards maintained a stranglehold on Mrs Chu which effectively disabled her mobility.

"I will not again remind you that you are still at the mercy of this court. If you treat the court once more with contempt, I will not hesitate to punish you. Do you understand?" The Judge reprimanded her.

Feeling pain around her arms, Mrs Chu replied in the affirmative, but once again thanked the Judge for solving her husband's murder.

But the Judge had more to say. "This Tribunal has not yet resolved your husband's murder case. It has merely reported that the two paintings lost from your residence have now been found in possession of the rice merchant. That is all."

"Your Honour, the Rice-merchant must have tried to swindle my husband. He apparently killed my husband by a blow-pipe filled with poison and stole two paintings. It was only through the will of Heaven that he was punished for the crime and died in the hotel fire. Now that the murderer had been found, my husband, the people of this town and I myself can live in peace, secure in our thoughts that the Tribunal acted appropriately and quickly...."

As Mrs Chu continued, the courtroom shouted their approval of the Judge. All now realized the connection between the Rice-merchant and the death of Fan-shing and how well blessed the town had been through the good will of Heaven and its gift to the town of a just and competent Judge. Even the usually reserved Candidate Soong joined in the shouts of joy.

Judge Quan grew increasingly tired of rapping with his gavel. He sat behind his bench, hands apart on the table, eyes focused on Mrs Chu. His face, tense with anger, now darkened and his eyes became sharp and piercing, giving him the appearance of a dragon ready to spew forth a flame of fire against all in the courtroom. Finally he succeeded in bringing the court back to order.

But then Mrs Chu spoke again. "Although I, myself, have been in a state of mourning, this town has too. For the past two days, we feared that the murderer might already have left town and would strike once more at will. Word spread that a murderer was amongst us and travelling merchants have begun to avoid the town. Businesses have not been doing well during these past two days. How long will it be before the Tribunal realizes that the townspeople have suffered enough? The real murderer was indeed the rice merchant. How else could he be in possession of my husband's stolen paintings?"

This speech aroused the whole courtroom. Murmurs changed to yells of protest as some people began to step forward but were prevented by the Tribunal guards. Mrs Chu had touched on the real issue. Businesses were slowing down and people were becoming more and more insecure. They, too, wanted an end to this case as much as Mrs Chu. It appeared that Candidate Soong also wanted the same, since he joined the crowd's protests against the Tribunal.

Judge Quan ordered the two guards who held Mrs Chu to let her go. As soon as she had been set free, she bowed once more to the Judge and wept again in protestation. Coroner Chen and E-Lung looked at each other, agitated and apprehensive, while Judge Quan remained motionless.

As the crowd attempted to move closer and closer to the bench, Coroner Chen gave a secret signal to E-Lung. They both immediately reached for their swords and pointed them at the approaching crowd. Both Coroner Chen and E-Lung stood in front of Judge Quan, ready to protect their master with their swords and their lives.   Their stance against the crowd had effectively blocked the Judge's view, but to his left, at the back of the court next to the pillar, the Judge saw the figure of Mrs Chu still slumped in a deliberately attention-seeking way on the floor. He then saw her lift her head, smile and than slowly drop her face down to the floor once more.

The sight of Mrs Chu smiling immediately stirred the Judge's memory. Suddenly he recalled the nightmare he had had a previous night of a young beautiful lady inviting him to step forth on to a bridge. He recalled that same woman laughing as he fell down into the dark abyss. It was the same laugh that he had heard from Mrs Chu, just moments ago. So this was the downfall Mrs Chu has planned for me, the Judge thought to himself.

Judge Quan immediately stood, picked up a wooden placard from the bench; threw it into the crowd and then reached for his own sword. The fallen placard now faced directly at the agitated crowd and read, "Execution by hanging." Those in front saw the placard and immediately stepped back in fear.

"Sergeant and Constable, execute anyone who dares come near!" the Judge shouted and pointed his large fingers at the crowds in front of him. As the screams and shouts began to subside, the Judge said in a thunderous voice, "I am still the Magistrate of Sui-chou. I am the representative of the August Moon Emperor of this great land. How dare you treat the Emperor's law with contempt? For inciting violence and false accusations against the Tribunal, twenty lashes will be imposed on Mrs Chu immediately." Then, speaking to Mrs Chu, he said, "For the duration of this case, Mrs Chu, you will be arrested and placed in the Tribunal's prison. Such contempt against this court has serious consequences. Your fate will be left to the Prefecture to decide."

The Judge threw the appropriate placard onto the floor. Two officers of the court immediately grabbed hold of Mrs Chu, and the twenty lashes were promptly imposed. Now that she had been arrested, Mrs Chu knew the Judge was free to resolve her husband's murder case unhindered. On the other hand, she also knew that her paramour, Candidate Soong, was on the outside. His influence was strong enough to create trouble for the Judge.

The Judge noticed that, even under torture, Mrs Chu showed no sign of struggle and pain. When the twenty lashes had been administered, the Judge ordered that she be dragged aside and given sour tea. Her presence was required for the next phase of the court proceedings.

"This court forms a crucial link in the Empire's judiciary system. The Emperor has placed upon me, as Magistrate, the task of governing justly over the people of this town. I am answerable only to the Prefecture. An attack of any form against this court is in effect an attack on the August Moon himself and that is why serious punishment is always meted out to those who even think of perpetrating such an act."

He sat back onto his seat, satisfied the people understood fully what he had just explained. He then spoke once more clearly to the court. "An autopsy will now be conducted on the rice merchant fire-victim. This court will prove to the people and to Mrs Chu that the merchant did not die in the hotel fire. Instead he was murdered."

CHAPTER ELEVEN

In only a few days, a just and brilliant Magistrate had become
embroiled in a complex murder case.

Behind his Tribunal desk, the Judge gave orders for the court to bring in a live piglet and a dead piglet. He also gave orders for two terracotta tubs and some wood to be brought to the court for a demonstration.

While the guards prepared the scene, the courtroom became silent. Everyone wondered what a live and dead animal had to do with Fan-shing and the burnt rice merchant case. Even Mrs Chu, smarting from her recent punishment, could only look at Candidate Soong inquisitively. For the first time, Judge Quan detected a connection between the two. Although it was a simple glance, it was enough to convince the Judge that the two were involved with each other.

As the dead piglet and the living piglet were brought into court, the guards placed some wood into each of the two terracotta tubs and the two pigs were each placed into a separate tub. Everyone could hear the high-pitched squeal of the live pig as Judge Quan gave orders for the wood to be lit.

The live pig's squealing was intolerable and most people in the court turned their faces away from the cruel scene of animal torture before them. In pursuit of justice, the Judge had chosen this demonstration as the only way he could prove to the people that closing the Fan-shing murder case, as requested so strongly by Mrs Chu, was at the least premature and at worst a miscarriage of justice.

Eventually, the deafening sounds of the dying pig gradually grew silent as the flame painfully consumed it. Judge Quan ordered the guards to put out the fire, while Coroner Chen prepared a table nearby to perform autopsies on the animals.

Coroner Chen started on the pig which was already dead before the fires had been lit. He walked around the table where the pig had already been placed. He reported to the Judge that the exterior skin of the pig was burnt beyond any value for examination. He asked the Judge if he could begin an internal examination of the pig, and the Judge agreed.

The Coroner took a long wooden implement, with a sharp scalpel fixed at the end. He opened the mouth of the pig with the scalpel, and with a candle in his other hand proceeded to cut a slice of skin from around the throat of the pig. The specimen cut was somewhat dried due to the intense flame, but it was nonetheless still flesh-red in color and unblemished by the flame. The cut specimen was then placed in a white bowl, marked as "specimen one".

The second pig was placed on the table and Coroner Chen repeated the previous procedure. This time he had a slight problem cutting a specimen slice of skin from the pig and when he finally did so, he placed dark and dried flesh onto a bowl, marked as "specimen two".

"Your Honour!" Coroner Chen began to make his report, "It appears that the dark and dried flesh of "specimen two" was caused by the animal breathing as it was consumed by the flame. The degree of colouration and dryness indicates that the pig breathed into the region of its throat the hot flame and cinders of the burning wood. Both factors contributed to the darkened nature of this specimen. In comparison, the first specimen, which is relatively still red in color, suggests that the pig was not breathing while it too was consumed in the flames. This proves that the animal from which the first specimen was extracted died before the flames were set."

When the Coroner finished his report on his findings, the two specimens were carried around the court for all to see. Mrs Chu looked at the Judge. In one simple demonstration, this Judge had proved that there was just cause not to close her husband's murder case. In doing so, he had destroyed her plan to bury her husband quickly and begin a life together with the Candidate.

Candidate Soong however, looked quietly at the demonstration. He kept his hands behind his back and stared away from the two specimens when they were paraded past him.

"Coroner, you may now proceed to examine the body of the rice merchant," the Judge announced.

While the Tribunal guards were bringing in the burnt body and placing it onto the examination table. Coroner Chen prepared himself with all the required implements to conduct the autopsy. Then, as usual, he walked around the body, poking certain parts with a stick. He knew that there was no value in examining the exterior parts of the body, but he also knew that the Judge wanted him to be thorough. As he worked, he said, "This fire-victim is a male in his late fifties or early sixties. It appears that the exterior of the skin has been badly burnt and I will immediately proceed to examine the victim's mouth."

The Coroner then carried out the same steps that he had taken with the pigs. Firstly, he opened the man's mouth, inserted a small, sharp knife between the space of the two missing front teeth and cut a specimen from the victim's throat. It took him some time but, eventually, the Coroner was able to take a piece of flesh out of the victim's mouth. It was black, dark and dry. The Coroner quickly placed it into a bowl and proceeded to extract another piece from the mouth. The Judge saw the specimen. In disbelief he descended from his bench, walked quickly over, and stood intently next to the Coroner.

Everyone in the courtroom wondered why the Judge took the unusual step of coming down from his bench. Few saw what had been extracted from the fire-victim, but all sat intently and patiently awaiting the Coroner's report.

Sweat flowed from the Coroner's forehead as he struggled with shaking hands to extract the next specimen. He began to cut a piece from a different section of the throat in the hope that the result would be different. Judge Quan held onto the Coroner's hands to calm him.

When the second piece was extracted, it too was similar to the first, dark and dry. The two specimens were then placed in the one bowl and paraded round for the people to see. Gasping noises could be heard around the courtroom.

In the meantime, Coroner Chen stood still and looked at Judge Quan in disbelief.

Judge Quan proceeded slowly back to his bench. E Lung gave the Judge a worried look as he walked past him and sat back onto his chair. The Judge could not make out what had gone wrong or how such a result could go against common sense. He sat there, with the whole courtroom below him, deep in silence. His melancholy face seemed paralyzed by the negative results of the examination.

Candidate Soong indicated that he wished to approach the bench. Judge Quan did not see him, but Coroner Chen signalled that he might do so.

"This insignificant person's name is Soong, only son of the first adviser to our illustrious Emperor." His voice interrupted the Judge's deep thoughts but when he heard the beginning of the Candidate's speech, he nodded for him to continue.

"Despite my limited studies in the judiciary system of this great land," the Candidate continued, "I have for many years been guided in the study of the law by my great father himself. I beg to defer to the Judge, but the Coroner's examination indicates that it was appropriate for the Rice-merchant to meet death for his cowardly act in killing Fan-shing and stealing his paintings. Heaven has judged the murderous Rice-merchant. It is now up to the Judge to heed Heaven's call and bring prompt justice to the Chu family."

Candidate Soong bowed deeply and respectfully three times for speaking so openly in court. The people in court also lowered their heads in regret at the court's prolonged investigation but were grateful that Candidate Soong had spoken on their behalf.

E-Lung looked at Coroner Chen. They did not know what the Judge would do next. The carefully worded speech from the Candidate mentioning his father's name meant that it would be difficult for the Judge to degrade the name of Soong if he decided to go against the Candidate's advice.

Judge Quan considered his next move, his body limp and motionless, his face dark and deeply tormented. No one dared to speak; not even Mrs Chu, struck dumb by the result of the autopsy on the Rice-merchant. She was proud of her paramour's speech and knew that it was better to stay still and quiet while her fate was being decided.

One thing was clear in the Judge's mind. Law and order in the town were of paramount importance to him. Judge Quan could control the people's rebellious actions in court. However, if at this moment he ignored the people's sufferings, further rebellious activities could occur beyond the Tribunal's control. Word would then leak out to the Prefecture. In a soft and solemnly slow voice the Judge finally spoke.

"I was appointed here by the August Moon to maintain justice in this town. If the townspeople have suffered in the course of the Tribunal's actions, the court apologizes. It appears that Rice-merchant He, a relative newcomer in this town, had a grudge against Fan-shing. He proceeded to steal two paintings from the

Chu residence and killed Fan-shing with White Cloud poison applied through a blow-pipe. He then handed the two paintings along with other items to the hotel for safe keeping and, since his enemy had been killed, he celebrated by drinking too much wine before proceeding back to his room. He boiled some water on the tea-stove and inadvertently fell asleep at the table in the middle of the room; the tea boiled over the hot coal and started the fire, which later consumed the entire hotel wing and the Rice-merchant himself.

"I will now draft these findings for the Prefecture and I will recommend that the Fan-shing murder case be closed. For the present, while the murder case is pending for closure, Mrs Chu will be released. As for the two stolen paintings, this court will hand them back to her immediately."

The Judge finished his summary as clearly and audibly as he could and than sat erect on his seat proudly for the whole court to see him.

For the first time, everyone felt sympathy for the Judge. In only a few days, a just and brilliant Magistrate had become embroiled in a complex murder case. All were stunned that the Judge could overlook the simple fact that the Rice-merchant was indeed the sole perpetrator of Fan-shing's murder. Obviously, the Judge was too inexperienced. Judge Quan sat passively behind his Tribunal desk and looked absent-mindedly ahead.

A Tribunal clerk approached the bench and handed the Judge a scroll pertaining to some routine matters. Judge Quan was aware of the clerk's presence and was suddenly startled when the town's Hotel Guild-Master walked clumsily into the courtroom, sweat running down his forehead. He shouted that a brawl had taken place at his hotel. Kneeling with great difficulty on the floor in front of Judge Quan, he quickly wiped his sweaty face with his long sleeve and bowed to the Judge. From his dais above, the Judge was somewhat amused at the somewhat porcine figure of the Guild-Master. He bit his tongue and reflected that this was a welcome break from the intense session he had just had on the Fan-shing murder case. He signalled for the Guild-Master to speak.

"Your Excellency, as you know, your subject's name is Sheng Lu-ching, operator and owner of several hotels in this blessed town of ours. Not long ago I was suddenly awakened from an afternoon sleep by a loud commotion outside of my hotel. My assistant rushed into the room and reported that there had been a brawl outside. I immediately rushed to the scene and to my horror, discovered a beggar's body lying face down on the ground in a pool of blood. Since the Warden was not there, I asked the crowd who had been responsible for such a violent act against a defenseless fellow. To my utter surprise everyone said it was my young new employee at the hotel. I swear to Your Excellency that he is now my ex-employee. My assistant hired him. It wasn't me. I would not in my…"

"What sort of injuries did this beggar suffer at the hand of your so-called former employee, Guild-Master? Where is the beggar and where is your former employee?" Judge Quan asked, purposely cutting short his subject's broadcast of his responsible behaviour in the absence of a Warden, as well as his blame of his assistant.

"Erhh, there was a large bruise on his forehead when we carried him from the street to the hotel. There was blood and he was unconscious. Your Excellency, he is in my hotel now. As to that no-good former employee, well that coward ran away and is nowhere to be seen. I swear in my ten years as an operator of a hotel…."

"That's enough Guild-Master. This courtroom is not your hotel. You may speak only if asked and answer only my questions, nothing else. Do you understand?"

"Yes, Your Excellency. I thought I'd come immediately and report…." The Guild-Master immediately placed his right hand over his mouth when he saw Judge Quan's frown and an officer approaching menacingly to reprimand him.

"I will summon the Coroner to your hotel, but until then, the well-being of this beggar will be under your care. Before you go, provide this Tribunal clerk with a brief description of the young man you employed and officers will be sent to arrest him. Now go and don't complain. Rich or poor, these people are still citizens of this town and you are under an obligation to assist when instructed to do so."

Judge Quan waved for the Guild-Master to leave and looked at him as he walked backwards, face down, front still facing the Judge. The judge smiled and reflected that, whoever the subject was, the Tribunal rules were strict and all subjects must adhere equally to them.

When the Guild-Master had left the courtroom, Judge Quan rapped with his gavel twice, determined not to deal with any further routine problems. He left the dais and began to walk towards the Tribunal library. The Judge knew that the Court's reputation and the trust he had tried to build with the people he governed was now in disarray.

CHAPTER TWELVE

You may call me what you like. A name is merely a fixed label put on an ever-changing body. How can one place a fixed name onto something that never remains the same?

E-Lung followed the Judge back to the Tribunal library. The Judge seemed to have lost his air of officialdom and integrity. Slumped in his chair and staring into the air, even the dragon insignia at the front of the Magistrate's robe looked somewhat subdued.

With a piece of red paper and a brush, Judge Quan proceeded to write to the Prefect. He wrote a detailed report, stating how the Fan-shing murder case had now been resolved and noting that the murderer had been accidentally killed in a hotel fire. The Judge concluded his letter stating that he awaited the Prefect's reply so that the murder case might officially be closed. Judge Quan then took the Tribunal's seal and stamped the piece of paper.

The Judge read the report to himself out loud and when he was satisfied he asked a Tribunal assistant to make several copies, which were to be placed outside the main gate for everyone to see, while the original was to be delivered to the Prefect immediately.

"Your Honour, I cannot help but notice that you have changed some facts in your report to the Prefect," E-Lung remarked. "In particular, about the Rice-merchant's death, you put down that he was killed accidently. Does Your Honour also believe that the Rice-merchant himself killed Fan-shing?" E-Lung asked inquisitively.

"The report will momentarily calm the local people. It will also appease Mrs Chu and Candidate Soong. I am even more convinced that both were involved in the murder of Fan-shing, in particular because of Mrs Chu's unusual criticism of the Tribunal and her courtroom theatrics. However, as the Tribunal has no hard evidence in its hands against the two of them, I have no choice but to release them. By recommending that the case be closed, I hope that both of our suspects will believe they are now free and that all their movements will be unhindered by the Tribunal. Since it may take several days for the Prefect to recommend that the case be closed, it will give this Tribunal extra time to continue its investigation in secret. Indeed, this report should appease everyone, including our suspects."

"I don't quite understand, Your Honour. We can't even prove that the Rice-merchant was murdered. Most of our evidence is, at best, circumstantial," E-Lung replied, apparently frustrated and tired.

A deep silence followed as Judge Quan tried to piece together all the evidence, but the tension and the disappointments from the court session had exhausted both these fighters against crime.

"I don't know, E-Lung," the Judge said. "But we must persist against the odds and only then will we become a little wiser and better then we were before. We are all inexperienced here. That is why we must persist while there is still time. We must learn from these difficulties and hopefully we will succeed in the end."

The two men each stepped forward towards the painting and each took a closer look at it again.

Then without any hesitation, the Judge spoke again. "E-Lung, you and I must immediately visit the hermit. I don't know what we may find there, but at least the fresh air and calmness of the mountains will clear my head." With these words, the Judge retired to his private chambers. It took some time before he re-appeared, wearing the same comfortable outfit that he had worn the previous night when he went to Mrs Chu's residence. The thin tunic was necessary, as the hot afternoon sun was now directly overhead. The two men put large round straw hats on their heads, both to protect them from the sun's rays and also to hide their identities.

The two men mounted their horses, now freed of any emblems that might indicate that they came from the Tribunal. Dressed as they were, in ordinary clothes, they should be able to blend in with the majority of the people.

E-Lung trotted in front of the Judge and guided his master's horse slowly out of the rear entrance of the Tribunal. He indicated to the Judge that no-one was present in the alley-way. The Judge then rode out of the Tribunal compound. Without a word, E-Lung took up a position in front of the Judge and kept some distance from him. They chose the shortest way out of town, along a route that led them to the river, over the bridge and out through the Western Gates, taking a path that gradually wound its way into the hills. The vegetation became denser and greener as they rode higher and higher. The hot afternoon sun was intermittently obscured by the thick foliage of the forest as their path narrowed and meandered upwards. The Judge felt the welcome coolness of the air and slowly began to relax. They climbed upwards for some time and when Judge Quan looked back he could see his town far below. He felt relieved and drawn to these hills, but at the same time he was ashamed to have left a town in trouble. Was he running away from his responsibilities? It took a while before the Judge could convince himself that this little expedition was required as part of the investigation and it was a means for both men to clear their minds and probably return to the town better able to resolve the murder case.

E-Lung kept up a constant but fast pace, realizing that it would be quite some time before they reached their destination. He kept his silence and continued to ride in front of the Judge.

At one point the road split into two directions. E-Lung led his horse along the right-hand path, confident that this was the correct way. Judge Quan realized once again how capable E-Lung was and how much his skills were an asset to the investigation. Apart from his apparent lack of fear and physical strength, he also had the intelligence to understand the complications of the Fan-shing murder case. His close relationship to the Coroner was also apparent to the Judge, who was happy that all three were working well together. The time they had spent together so far had strengthened and cemented their relationships.

"Aren't you afraid of meeting the hermit and perhaps losing track of time?" asked the Judge as he slowly guided his horse alongside E-Lung's.

"As an ex-officer of the military, I saw and fought in many campaigns. Nothing can compare to fighting against the Mongolian hordes up north. But Your Honour has freed me from military service. For this I am forever in your debt."

As he bowed to the Judge, Judge Quan also bowed low, not to E-Lung, but to avoid hitting his head against a low-lying branch that obstructed the road. The two men broke into loud laughter and E-Lung caught a glimpse of the Judge's light-heartedness.

Just as quickly as it came, however, the Judge's face returned to its usual serious expression, as he continued to speak. "I don't want you to follow me across the bridge."

E-Lung was about to protest but the Judge cut him short. "This is my search; my discovery, I must do it alone. You must guard the bridge while I am away"

E-Lung stifled his protests and obeyed the Judge's orders. Although he would have liked to accompany the Judge to protect him, he knew that in the past few days Judge Quan had lost something that was valuable to him. His ideals and his will to serve had been all but shattered by the rebellious people of the town. E-Lung realized that this trip into the mountains was being made, not only to enable the Judge to investigate the bridge and any connection that it might have to the murder case. It was also an opportunity for the Judge to find himself.

Before long they came out into a clearing and saw the broken suspension bridge ahead. E-Lung was right, thought the Judge. The scene here bore little or no resemblance to Fan-shing's painting. There was no pavilion; nor did the bridge lead to a view of a lush green plain and a meandering river. Rather, the view was dominated by hundreds of trees that were divided beyond the bridge by a road that curved around itself and disappeared over the next hill.

Suddenly, a gentle breeze sprang up and the Judge felt its soothing coolness against his body. As the Judge and E-Lung dismounted from their horses and focused their attention on the bridge, the Judge told himself that this was a reasonably inviting site.

It was an old bridge, crudely made with a few wooden planks fastened with an aging series of ropes. The ropes were fastened to wooden pillars carved with faint writing. It was obvious that travelling merchants had once used this bridge, but the route had long since been abandoned and the structure had been allowed to deteriorate. It hung slightly to one side, loosened by many years of neglect and swayed gently in the cool breeze.

Judge Quan moved forward and looked at the scene below the bridge. There was a long, seemingly endless drop down into a deep ravine. He immediately stepped away, frightened not only by the depth below, but by the memories of his nightmare which came rushing back.

In his dream, he was drawn to the bridge by a female figure. Now he was near to the bridge and he felt compelled to cross it. But the fall in his dream had made him overly sensitive and doubts soon began to grip his mind.

Sensing the Judge's hesitation, E-Lung slowly walked onto the edge of the bridge. He looked down and then walked further out into the middle of the bridge. Looking back at the Judge, he jumped up and down, creating a loud squeaking noise as the rope torsion increased its grip on the eroding wooden planks. He then walked back to the Judge without any difficulty.

Judge Quan put his hands onto E-Lung's shoulder and smiled. "If you ever do anything as foolish as that again, I will send you back to the military."

Then the Judge realized that he had let his emotions get the better of him. He must think rationally. The fall from the bridge was only in a dream caused by fear. If he didn't cross the real bridge now to see the hermit, he might suffer a greater downfall at the hands of Mrs Chu and perhaps others as well.

With that thought in mind, the Judge gave quick instructions to E-Lung to guard the bridge. He then took a first careful step onto the structure. The wooden planks squeaked loudly as he took his first steps. He turned around to face E-Lung. "That did not happen to you when you took the first step," he said jokingly, partly to contain his own fear as he continued to walk forward.

Without looking down, he focused his attention on the task ahead. The bridge began to sway sideways as the Judge increased his pace. Fearful that the bridge would not hold any longer, he made a final leap and planted both feet firmly on the other side. He gave a loud sigh of relief as he looked back at E-Lung, raising his hands to acknowledge that all was well. Looking forward, he continued to walk up the hill and disappeared from E-Lung's view.

The Judge increased his pace as he continued into the woods. Shafts of sunlight illuminated a narrow path overgrown by thick vegetation. As the path descended, the Judge descended with it. From a distance, he could smell what appeared to be burning incense and this encouraged him to believe that the hermit was nearby. Quickly he increased his pace.

Suddenly, the path came to a dead end, completely blocked by trees and grass. The only way forward seemed to be by a set of crudely made steps, which led to a further descent.

The Judge started down the steps immediately, his sense of urgency increasing as the smell became stronger. He was unafraid. Rather he felt strongly that the answers he sought lay in front of him. It was an unusual and compelling feeling.

The set of steps twisted several times before they came to an end. Beyond, the Judge could hear the flow of running water. The smell of incense was probably at its strongest. He felt frustrated and exhausted. In the past few days, other people had controlled his actions; first, Mrs Chu; then Candidate Soong and, finally, the people of the town. Now perhaps it was going to be this hermit whom he had made this difficult journey to see.

The Judge's anger grew as he turned and faced the cliff, banging his frustrated hands against the thick, overhanging vegetation, but suddenly he fell headlong into darkness. He found himself tumbling down a long flight of stone steps and eventually landed on a cold, flat but rough floor.

The pain in his head was excruciating as he attempted to see where he had fallen. He rubbed his forehead with both hands in an attempt to soothe the pain. But he immediately realized that this was the only bodily damage he had sustained from the fall. He stood up, cursed himself for his clumsiness and peered around his surroundings.

He was in a large and dark cave. The blue mist ahead was strange but comforting when the Judge realized that there was also a source of light beyond it. He walked forward and experienced a heightened sense of self, becoming aware of every bodily action. His breathing, his heartbeat, his sight and his leg movements ... he was aware of them all and felt an unusual oneness with himself.

As he walked further forward, the unmistakable smell of incense became stronger. Blinded by the mist, the Judge walked in the direction of the light. Soon he came out of the mist and into a large circular cavern, lit by four torches which hung on the cavern walls.

In the middle of the cavern, water in a large cauldron was being kept on the boil with the help of a small fire fed by a few large pieces of wood. The liquid was overflowing onto the floor and as it touched the cold ground it immediately turned into the "mist" the Judge had previously walked through.

To his right, there was a raised platform adorned with a red cushion and a large floor-mat, indicating that the platform was being used for meditation. To his left was a hastily-made table that bore a few scrolls and brushes. The scrolls were so old that the Judge could barely recognize the writings. Apart from these, there was nothing else in the cavern and no sign of the hermit.

The hermit's absence did not bother the Judge for he began to experience a feeling of exhaustion. His head began to spin and his body seemed no longer able to support his weight as he fell into a deep sleep.

It was some time before the Judge rose from his sleep, evidently awakened by the same strong smell of incense. He adjusted his eyes with both hands and noticed in front of him a male figure sitting in a full lotus meditation position. The man wore a loose white tunic and had long straight hair. Since his back was towards him, the Judge could not make out any facial features. He decided, however, to copy the hermit and sit on the ground in a similar position.

It was not long before the hermit turned to face the Judge. As he did so, the Judge bowed his head and said, apologetically, "Forgive me for intruding," while raising his head to look at the old hermit for the first time. He was immediately taken aback, since he had seen this man before. Though the man's hair was untied, his face was smoother now in the semi-darkness of the cavern. It was the old noodle-cart pusher from the previous night, the man he had paid for the loan of his cart.

The old hermit saw the Judge's reaction, smiled and bowed to the Judge.

"I welcome Your Honour to my humble residence. It is an honour to be blessed by your visit."

Judge Quan quickly raised the hermit's shoulders. "The honour is certainly mine," he replied. "As you are a man who has renounced the world and taken the spiritual path, let us do away with the customary formalities."

"I have no need for material things. I have given all the silver pieces you gave me to a needy beggar at the Southern Gate of Your Honour's town. I hope Your Honour will approve," the Hermit said apologetically.

"Certainly it was ignorant of me not to know that you were a learned and wise man. May I inquire Your Reverence's name?" the Judge asked.

"You may call me what you like. A name is merely a fixed label put on an ever-changing body. How can one place a fixed name onto something that never remains the same?"

Judge Quan nodded. It was true; our physical self is never constant. Our thoughts change; our hair grows and falls and our sight fails with age. We are not in control of our bodies. They are indeed transient and therefore there is no meaning in giving something so impermanent a fixed name.

The old hermit smiled again, knowing that the Judge had understood what he had just said. He continued, "For many years I have lived in the town that is now under your jurisdiction. I still have a vested interest in the well-being of the people. I make an impromptu visit to the town whenever a new Magistrate arrives. Lately, I heard that Your Honour was in town, so I disguised myself as a noodle-cart pusher. When I saw you last night, I knew immediately that you will bring much happiness and justice to the people."

Judge Quan wondered whether to ask the old hermit some questions about the murder case, but the old hermit continued. "I know that you are experiencing some difficulties. What is life without suffering? Much can be learned from it. But sometimes one needs to stand above suffering and see its true nature. Then suffering will no longer be our enemy, but our friend."

The old hermit paused and pointed at the old and worn-out books in the cavern. "I spent many years in the study of Taoism and alchemy. Eventually, one realizes that all such teachings serve merely to bring one into harmony with one's surroundings, and that all this is achieved by thought. I have gone beyond those teachings, so why cling onto them? If I grasp them, they will not take me further; they will in fact be a burden. This realization itself began from a thought."

When the old hermit had finished, he smiled at Judge Quan. The Judge felt that the hermit knew why he was here Although he did not fully comprehend all that the old man had said, he felt honoured to be in the presence of the wise old sage.

The Judge bowed his head respectfully, thanking the hermit for his teachings. When he lifted his head, the old man was nowhere to be seen. The steam that drifted from where the old sage had previously been sitting slowly passed away and was absorbed in the cauldron of boiling liquid. Once more, the Judge was left alone in the cavern.

He felt as if a weight had been lifted from his shoulders. In the hermit's presence, the Judge had experienced a sense of inner peace and contentment, the like of which he had never known before. For the first time he realized he had been too impatient during the murder case. In his drive to resolve his first serious challenge, he had made the error of paying too much attention to Mrs Chu's initial grief. That had caused him to conduct an incomplete investigation of the woman's house. Furthermore, when matters did not go his way, anger had often clouded his judgement. Now aware of this, Judge Quan felt rejuvenated and resolved to continue the murder investigation. This time he, and not Mrs Chu, would dictate it.

The Judge rose from his knees, bowed three times and backed respectfully out of the cavern. From there, he quickly left the cave and trudged back to the mountain. He looked up and realized the sun had already set, but there was just enough light left for him to make his way back to the bridge.

E-Lung was awakened by a loud cracking noise as the Judge crossed the wooden bridge, this time without hesitation.

"Your Honour, you have been away for a long time. Did you find the old hermit?" E-Lung asked half-heartedly, as he rubbed his eyes with both hands.

"I have not been away for long. It is only nightfall. I took a short nap before I met the old hermit," the Judge said triumphantly.

"Your Honour, it is not nightfall; it is now sunrise. You were away for the whole of last night."

Judge Quan looked at E-Lung, surprised and bewildered. Had he really been away for that long? The Judge looked at the sky in the direction of the sun and saw that it was indeed rising slowly above the horizon.

Interlude

The sun cast its early warning rays onto the still town of Sui-chou. A blanket of thick fog hung over the river. Out of the silence came a lone man, struggling with two large sacks on his back. He headed towards the river and moments later reappeared, freed from his heavy load, and walked back to the still and lifeless township.

CHAPTER THIRTEEN

Revenge from beyond, indeed!

When Judge Quan and E-Lung approached the town's Western Gate, it was still closed. Unwilling to reveal their true identity in case word got out that the Tribual was still conducting an investigation into the Fan-shing murder case, E-Lung had to bang on the gate and convince the guard that they had come early to town to do some business as rice merchants. After a heated exchange, the guard reluctantly let them through.

At the Tribunal, the drum had begun to roll for the morning court session. Coroner Chen greeted the Judge and E-Lung warmly and somewhat excitedly. The Judge thought it was unusual for the Coroner to be so lively, but there was little time to talk.

Judge Quan looked around his court and noted with satisfaction the absence of Mrs Chu and Candidate Soong. Evidently, they must have thought that the Judge had officially closed the Fan-shing murder case. The crowds on the public benches were curious to see what the Judge would do next.

"I, Magistrate of Sui-chou, have sent a letter to the Prefect recommending that the Fan-shing murder case be closed. This letter is available for all to see outside the Tribunal. It is hoped that this action will soon restore business confidence in the town."

Judge Quan quickly rapped twice with the gavel to close the morning court session. It was short, simple and direct. He remained seated until most of the people had filed out of court, in case someone wished to make an impromptu complaint to the Court as had happened in the past few days. Satisfied that there were no more new cases to deal with, the three men returned to the Tribunal library.

The Judge told his two assistants what had transpired during his visit to the old hermit. He explained some of the things the hermit had told him and said that although he did not fully understand the hermit's teachings, he was nonetheless much more determined and looked forward to resolving the murder case swiftly. He explained that through his inexperience and impatience, he had let his emotions cloud his judgement. From

94

now on, he would be more careful and prudent in his task as a Judge. He concluded by saying that he had been with the old hermit only for a short while. Although he had taken a nap, he felt that that itself did not account for the long duration of the visit.

Both Coroner Chen and E-Lung felt that the Judge looked more relaxed and less strained after the visit to the old hermit. Perhaps this visit had in some way allowed the Judge to rediscover himself and his passion for the Judiciary system.

After the Judge had completed his recollections, Coroner Chen began to speak. "I followed the Guild-Master back to his hotel in town after yesterday's court session. He is quite a character, despite the brawl and the fire at his hotel. He spoke of his plan to open a fourth hotel in the more affluent north-eastern part of this town and he tried to persuade me to recommend this to Your Honour, in order to receive the approval of the Tribunal. But I ignored his request.

"As for the beggar, he had suffered an intense blow, possibly a kick on his forehead. His skin was cut and bleeding had resulted. During my examination, he drifted in and out of consciousness. His name is still unknown to us. Normally, such a blow would not be fatal, but beggars are normally frail and I fear for his health. The next two to three days are critical. I have set his death limit to five days. If he does recover, he should do so fully in that time."

The Judge looked out of the window, not really paying any attention to the activities outside. He reminded himself that a "Death limit" normally meant that the injured person is handed back to his attacker to allow him to nurse the victim back to health. Otherwise, the victim's relatives might threaten to kill or extort money from the attacker. This had happened before on numerous occasions. Of course, the assailant might want to help his victim so that on the expiration of the death limit, he could possibly avoid further prosecution, or the death penalty. In most cases, the death limit was meant to save the lives of both the attacker and his victim. In this situation, however, the attacker – the ex-employee – was still at large.

"When I returned from the hotel," Coroner Chen continued, "I had little to do in the way of duty so I took the liberty of paying an impromptu secret visit to Mrs Chu's residence during the evening. It occurred to me that during our investigations at Mrs Chu's residence, we had been there for only a short period of time. I was determined this time to stay there for as long as it took, to find out exactly what goes on at the house. So I climbed to the same place that Your Honour did previously.

"There was no activity on the second level of the house. I could however see some light coming from a bottom window, where I understood Mrs Chu usually taught her dance classes. I decided to climb down and hide underneath the window, which was slightly open. "At first, I dared not look inside but I could hear Mrs Chu's voice. She wasn't crying or mourning; rather she was singing softly to herself and I could see that she was packing some wooden crates. She must have thought that the Tribunal had given up and that she was free to leave town after her husband's burial.

"Then Mrs Chu's solitary singing stopped and two more voices joined hers. They must have been guests who had invited themselves in, as I did not hear Mrs Chu leave the room to open the door. The two voices were not unfamiliar and one of them sounded very much like Candidate Soong. I decided to kneel down and peer through the partially opened window.

"Sure enough, I could see Candidate Soong speaking to Mrs Chu. His normally reserved and academic manner was absent. Instead, he seemed to be nervous as he tried to calm both Mrs Chu and a second man, whom both he and Mrs Chu addressed as 'Warden'. The discussion turned into an argument as Mrs Chu shouted that she had paid the Warden enough money already."

"You mean the Warden I scolded the other day at Mrs Chu's place? Was he there?" The Judge was surprised that a third person was now also involved.

"Yes, Your Honour, the same...."

Returning to his main topic, Coroner Chen continued: "Candidate Soong seemed to be really nervous. I could sense this, when he came to the window to shut it tightly. For a moment I thought I was going to be caught, but luck was on my side. He must have been so preoccupied with the problem they were discussing that he failed to see me hiding outside.

"Although I couldn't see inside the room, I knew who the involved parties were. So, I just sat there and listened quietly. It transpired that the Warden wanted more money and Mrs Chu refused. In the ensuing argument, Candidate Soong told Mrs Chu to lower her voice but this only served to increase her anger and she struck the Candidate. There was a long silence and finally the Warden said that if he did not receive the extra money he would go to the Judge and tell all. By now, Candidate Soong was very agitated. He must have feared that their plan was about to crumble and he begged Mrs Chu to give in. He was almost in tears when Mrs Chu finally said that she would have the money in a few days time. "Then I could hear only two voices, so I suspected that the Warden had left. I could hear Mrs Chu scolding Candidate Soong for giving in so easily to the Warden's ridiculous demands. The Candidate didn't reply. Then I heard Mrs Chu say that she was only buying more time. She would never give the money to the Warden. They would be out of the town before they needed to pay the money."

"What happened next?" the Judge asked.

"That good-for-nothing woman must have been proud of herself, for she began to dance and sing to the Candidate. I think they both enjoyed it because I heard laughter coming from the two of them. And all this was happening while Fan-shing's body was still in the house."

"I knew that old Warden was incompetent when he did such a half-hearted job of guarding Mrs Chu's residence before I arrived to inspect Fan-shing's body." Following these words, Judge Quan looked at Coroner Chen expecting confirmation, but noticed the Coroner's strange stare.

"But Your Honour, the Warden I saw last night was a young man. I had never seen him before last night, certainly not at Mrs Chu's residence," Coroner Chen said, looking at the Judge, then at E-Lung and then at the Judge again.

Judge Quan sat there, silent and motionless, except that his right hand constantly caressed his short beard. Not sure what to make of the Judge's reaction, the Coroner decided to pour the three of them a cup of tea.

While the Coroner was pouring the tea, the Judge suddenly stood up and slammed both his hands on the table with such a loud bang that the noise must have been heard outside the library. The Coroner was so startled by this that he accidentally dropped the teapot which broke into pieces. Hot tea poured out onto the floor and down the Coroner's clothes.

Judge Quan was staring at Fan-shing's painting and with one finger pointing at it, spoke excitedly. "This painting started it all. I knew that my nightmare and the painting were linked. It wasn't until E-Lung mentioned the bridge then I finally saw the connection between this painting and my nightmare. Since the nightmare was also about a vile female, it suggested to me that Mrs Chu was embroiled in her husband's murder case. But so far all the evidence has been mere theory. There was nothing that could be used in court."

Both Coroner Chen and E-Lung nodded in agreement.

"This painting that was done so diligently by Fan-shing during his last days was in a style that he rarely used. He must have known that his wife was planning something against him. Look at the shape of the river meandering through the plain, followed by the three animals forming a line below the river and then the two rows of trees leading up to the mountain. Put together, they form a word."

Judge Quan paused and looked at his two assistants, waiting for a response.

Coroner Chen thought for a while and than slapped E-Lung on the shoulders. "That's right! As I understand it, Mrs Chu's full name was Chu Hong-li. The word Hong means red and red is written as such in Fan-shing's painting. Mrs Chu's name is on the painting."

"Revenge from beyond, indeed!" Judge Quan smiled. "This gives us the first direct link between Mrs Chu and the murder case which we can use in court. Fan-shing suspected that his wife would kill him all along. Unable to report the crime, he left a brilliant clue in the form of a painting, to await a Magistrate who could solve the artist's murder. The next link is Candidate Soong, who, as Coroner Chen's observation last night proves, is indeed also connected to the case.

"Yes, Your Honour, Fan-shing was very clever," continued the Coroner. "The victim provided a clue in such a way that his wife could not have spotted it, but still gave enough for Your Honour to discover it. But what I can't understand is why Fan-shing didn't report the plot and save his own life? Why create such an elaborate plan?"

"You have just said the word, Coroner Chen – 'clever' – " replied the Judge. "Fan-shing knew his wife was plotting against him and he also knew that Candidate Soong was involved. He knew of Soong's reputation and his official connections. Fanshing knew also that if he had reported his case, the Judge of the day, namely my predecessor, would have dismissed it in court. No official papers would be produced in court because my predecessor must have been bought over by the Candidate."

"How can you say that, Your Honour?" Coroner Chen replied angrily, since he had worked in a limited capacity as Coroner for the previous Judge, and had found him to be an honest and righteous man.

Realizing that he might have offended Coroner Chen; the Judge quickly clarified his statement. "We know that Candidate Soong hardly ever studied and yet he was able to pass the local examination with excellent grades. Such exams were always administered and supervised by the local Magistrate. One way to obtain a favourable outcome for the exam results would be to obtain the favour of the Magistrate. The fact that my predecessor has left our town along with all other local examiners also points to this fact."

Judge Quan paused. Then, "Coroner Chen!" the Judge continued, "Did you not say that the Warden you saw arguing with Mrs Chu last night was a young man?"

Coroner Chen nodded affirmatively.

"E-Lung, during our investigation of the hotel room where the Rice-merchant was found, you left that room under my orders to fetch the Hotel Guild-Master. Was that young Warden still standing outside that room?"

E-Lung nodded assent.

"And yet I had told that Warden that he had done an excellent job and that he was allowed to go home for a well-earned rest. I told him this before we went into the room. Why was he still around?" The Judge asked. When no-one answered, he continued. "That young Warden was the same Warden whom Coroner Chen saw last night."

Seeing that his assistants were bewildered, Judge Quan walked to the window and peered outside. After a few quiet moments, the Judge turned to face his assistants:

"When E-Lung left the hotel room to fetch the Guild-Master, I was myself examining the Rice-merchant's throat. I saw that the flesh was not dark or charred but still slightly red. That was why I had the demonstration carried out with the two pigs, I was confident that the Rice-merchant's specimen would indicate that he died before the fire was set. But then Coroner Chen proved otherwise!"

Judge Quan looked away and breathed a heavy sigh. "If I had been more experienced, I could have come to this conclusion earlier, but I was so caught up with Mrs Chu's slanderous accusations that I couldn't see the connection."

"What connection?" E-Lung asked, unable to understand what the Judge was saying.

"The Warden was obviously bribed by the Candidate. When he saw that I was onto something with the Rice-merchant's throat, he quickly switched the body with that of another person who had really died by fire."

"You mean there could be a third body? Another murder?" asked E-Lung, now even more perplexed. Coroner Chen began to smile and explained, "The Warden switched the body before he brought it to the Tribunal. A clever plan! He knew Mrs Chu's theatrics in court would force the Judge to conduct an autopsy quickly. That meant that either I or the Judge would not have enough time to conduct a preliminary check and validate that it was the correct body. By the time I conducted the autopsy, it was too late. The body had already been switched and we did not realize it.

"Now the Warden is demanding more money from Mrs Chu because he was a party to yet another murder. He also set fire to a hotel belonging to a prominent citizen,"

"Yes," said the Judge. "I'm sure you're right." Then, turning to the other man, he said, "E-Lung, bring me a map of the township and a recent list of missing people."

E-Lung was about to exit the library, when he stopped and turned to speak to the Judge. "But Your Honour, we can't rely on Coroner Chen's evidence alone. He is in the service of the Court and his evidence might be seen by the Prefect to be biased against the case."

Judge Quan and Coroner Chen looked at each other as the library door closed behind E-Lung. Both knew that there was a degree of truth in what he had said. The Judge walked impatiently round the library twice and then said to the Coroner:

"We must act quickly or else they might dispose of the real Rice-merchant's body. We would then lose our only means of implicating Mrs Chu. E-Lung is right. We can't use your evidence. It seems to me that that young Warden may be the weak link in a clever murder plot. It appears, from what we know now, that he was frightened by his involvement. If we can get to this young Warden we might very well be able to get to the others."

When E-Lung returned, Judge Quan asked him to read out the number of men reported missing. When E-Lung answered "Four," the Judge then asked how many had been reported missing since the hotel fire.

"Only one of the four men, Your Honour. Someone named Shao," E-Lung answered.

"What?" Judge Quan slammed his hands against the library table. "You mean Examiner Shao has been reported as missing?" He looked at Coroner Chen.

"Yes, Your Honour," said E-Lung. "It appears that the Examiner's neighbours were worried when they didn't see him perform his regular Tai Chi exercise. They notified their local Warden, who in turn knocked on the Examiner's front door. When there was no response, he forced open the door and searched the house. Examiner Shao was nowhere to be found. The Warden subsequently reported him missing to the Tribunal."

Adding to E-Lung's report, the Coroner said: "Your Honour, I should have made the connection yesterday during the examination of the fire-victim's body. I noticed several of the victim's front teeth missing, a feature I observed when I visited Examiner Shao. I did not pay much attention during the examination. I was too preoccupied with extracting the throat specimen. But come to think of it, they were the same missing teeth," said the Coroner, as he turned and looked at the Judge. "The Rice Merchant's body that your Honour examined at the Guild-Master's hotel must have been replaced by the body of Examiner Shao."

"Show me the map of the town, E-Lung!" ordered the Judge. The Judge's assistant unrolled a map on a convenient table. The Judge and the Coroner moved closer to examine the map.

"This is the Guild-Master's hotel, next to the river. Here is the Tribunal. Between these two places lies the body of the real

Rice-merchant." As he spoke, the Judge moved his finger from the hotel, along the road to the bridge over the river and to the Tribunal. He continued to mark this route several times. Then, without a word, he slammed his hand onto the table.

"The body must be in the river or nearby. The river flows from the North to the South of town. If anyone were to dispose of a body, it would have to be between the hotel location where the fire took place and downstream towards the southern wall.

"Coroner Chen!" he ordered then. "Recruit as many men as possible and split them into two groups. One group should begin the search in the river near the hotel; the other should begin from the southern wall moving upstream. With any luck, the narrowing of the river channel will have prevented the body from being carried out of town."

As Coroner Chen left the library to organize the search-party, Judge Quan turned to E-Lung.

"I want you to arrest that young Warden and place him in the Tribunal prison cell. We may not yet have direct evidence to link him to the murder, but we can bring him into court on the pretext that there are some follow-up questions regarding the hotel fire. Go now, quickly!"

E-Lung quickly left the library, leaving the Judge alone.

Sitting behind his desk, the Judge took out a piece of red paper and with his tongue wet the tip of an ink brush. He then proceeded to write a formal letter to Candidate Soong. Since the murder case was pending for closure, he wrote, he had finally found the time to pay a formal visit to the Candidate. At the end of the letter, the Judge wrote, "Magistrate of Sui-chou in the Ch'eng-tu Prefecture of the Chien-nan Province of the Illustrious Tang Empire," and this signature on his letter he then imprinted with the official Tribunal stamp.

Then the Judge gave the letter to a messenger, ordering him to deliver it immediately to Candidate Soong. After receiving this formal letter, the Candidate would not dare to leave the town before Judge Quan's visit.

That left Mrs Chu. He ordered two guards to watch over her residence. They were to keep a close watch over the house. If she left the house, they were to arrest her immediately.

With both Mrs Chu and the Candidate taken care of, the Judge made preparations to join the search by the river. This time, eager finally to expose the cruel and merciless murder of Fan-shing by his wife and her paramour, he decided not to change out of his Magistrate's clothes.

CHAPTER FOURTEEN

I am indeed glad that you could pay the Soong residence a visit, Judge Quan Wu-meng. There is nothing so good as leaving the stifling walls of a Tribunal and being out among the people you were placed to govern.

The Judge's horse galloped quickly towards the bridge over the river. Everyone who saw the Judge, clad in his full Magistrate's attire, was immediately aware that something significant was to take place.

The morning sun had almost reached its highest point in the sky as it shone down onto the river, making it glisten like thousands of sparkling diamonds. It was a perfect day to be out of the Tribunal, thought the Judge, as he guided his horse onto the bridge. From here, he could see that the search-party had already begun in earnest.

Two large river barges were being slowly rowed alongside each other, the men on board using long poles to search the river bottom, in the hope of hitting anything which resembled a body. Intermittently, one of the men would indicate a certain spot and another man would dive underneath the water for a closer look. After some time, he would re-emerge and indicate that nothing had been found.

At the same time another search-party was combing the river-bank. Some men were wading in the water just above knee-height, while others were looking underneath abandoned logs and rocks. So far, there had been no result.

The Judge guided his horse towards the hotel. Along the way he was joined by E-Lung. The Constable's presence indicated to the Judge that he had already placed the Warden under arrest and Judge Quan looked at E-Lung in surprise.

In response, E-Lung spoke to the Judge with a grin on his face. "It seems that our young Warden was scared out of his wits when he realized that he was being arrested. With a little persuasion in the form of torture, I'm sure he'll tell us the truth."

The Judge patted E-Lung on the shoulders.

At the hotel, the Guild-Master was surprised to see the Judge.

Judge Quan indicated to him that he would like to go upstairs where he could have a better view of the river. The Hotel

Guild Master escorted the Judge up the stairs and ordered one of his assistants to clear the whole floor so that the Judge could be alone.

As Judge Quan stood on the balcony, which afforded an excellent view of the river, he noticed that there was already a small crowd gathered by the bank of the river, interested in what the Tribunal search-party was doing.

"Where is the Coroner?" The Judge asked E-Lung, who had joined the Judge and was also surveying the scene.

"The last I heard he was still downstream conducting the search. We should be able to see him as the search-party moves upstream."

"E-Lung, take some men and clear those townspeople from the river bank!" the Judge ordered. "I don't want anyone to come close to the crime scene."

E-Lung bowed and went back down the stairs.

"May I ask the Judge what the search-party is looking for?"

The Judge turned to his left and noticed the fat Guild-Master with a smile on his face. "Your burnt and dead Rice-merchant", he answered abruptly. "Now what else do you want to know about Tribunal business?" he barked, more annoyed by the Guild-Master than by the increasingly curious crowd now gathered by the river.

The Guild-Master saw the Judge's annoyance; quickly poured him a cup of tea and turned to leave.

"Wait!" Judge Quan motioned for the Guild-Master to sit next to him. "How is our beggar friend doing?" he asked.

"Well, he's much better now, Your Excellency," the Guild-Master replied, slowly taking his seat, and wondering why the Judge was suddenly showing him some degree of kindness. "But," he continued, "Last night, he was feverish. He kept screaming aloud, wanting more rice continuously. I thought he was hungry so I had some rice brought in for him, but he only pushed it away. What gratitude! A beggar will always be a beggar.

"I think his fever has broken and this morning he could eat and speak normally. The medicine prescribed by your Coroner helped immensely. But I also believe that setting a death limit of five days was a bit too much. In just one morning, he has eaten enough of my hotel food to sustain one of my customers for five days." The Guild-Master spoke as if desperate to rid himself of the beggar but being unable to do so under the provision of the death limit law.

"Ask one of my guards to take him to the Tribunal," the Judge replied. "He will from this day onwards be under the Tribunal's care."

The Guild-Master bowed several times to thank the Judge before he took his leave. He also smiled, knowing that the beggar was now safely in the Tribunal's custody.

Soon E-Lung returned and rejoined the Judge. By now the sun had moved past its highest point in the sky. The day had become increasingly hot and humid as the Judge and E-Lung observed the search-party working diligently. The two men noticed that the search-party from downstream was working slowly towards the hotel and they both saw Coroner Chen galloping towards the hotel.

When the Coroner arrived and sat at a table next to the Judge, sweat ran freely from his forehead as E-Lung poured him a cup of tea. The Coroner drank it in one mouthful and asked for another.

"We worked slowly from the river downstream and so far we've found no body whatsoever." He paused for a while to drink a second cup.

"I had a second search-group row a barge behind the first group. Still we found nothing...I am afraid, if it was in the water, the body may by now..."

"The body is still in the river, said the Judge firmly. "Direct that second group to the northern wall and ask them to search downstream towards the hotel. Make sure they pay careful attention to the farm sector, as silt in the water there will make the search more difficult."

Coroner Chen and E-Lung began to leave. They had almost reached the stairs when the Judge suddenly stopped them and asked them to wait for him on the bridge.

Once there, the three men looked on at the efforts of the search-party.

The Judge became increasingly impatient and annoyed. It was imperative that they find the body, as it was the only evidence that the Court would ever have to link Mrs Chu, Candidate Soong and the Warden to Fan-shing's murder. Standing there, slowly stroking his beard, "Hand me the map, E-Lung!" he suddenly asked.

E-Lung took the scrolled map from his loose tunic and unfurled it on the floor of the bridge, letting the hot sun scorch the paper. Then all three men grouped together looking at the map.

"Look," the Judge said, "We are here. As far as I can see there are no abandoned houses or temples between the hotel and the Tribunal, so the body must be in the river somewhere!" The Judge looked at E-Lung for confirmation, brushing the flies from his face.

"Could the body be here in the farm sector where it is more secluded?" asked E-Lung, slapping his hands on his neck in a vain attempt to kill the many flies that had suddenly begun to pester him.

"No, it is too far from the hotel and the Tribunal. The Warden must have temporarily disposed of the body," said the Judge. The persistent flies irritated and tested the Judge's patience even further and then suddenly he shouted out, "Why are there so many flies on..."

"... the bridge?" Coroner Chen completed the other's thought excitedly, and all three men looked at each other.

E-Lung was the first to move. He ran back in the direction of the hotel, and before he reached the end of the bridge, looked over and saw how the low tide revealed the river bed beneath the bridge. He jumped off the bridge and landed on the soft ground. His feet sank deep into the mud as he struggled to move around underneath the bridge.

There he noticed two partially-submerged rice-sacks. They were secured to the river-bed by a large wooden pole. Flies were swarming round the sacks in their hundreds. E-Lung struggled against the insects as he ran to the sacks and attempted to kick the pole away. But it wasn't until Coroner Chen joined E-Lung that they succeeded in removing the pole from the sacks. E-Lung then lifted both sacks and hoisted them onto his back. They were heavy due to their contents and their water-logged state. Then both he and Coroner Chen struggled along the soft river-bed back to the Judge.

Coroner Chen helped E-Lung unload the heavy sacks on the ground next to the bridge. Already there was a strong stench of decay emanating from the sacks, as Coroner Chen and E-Lung opened them with their knives. When the sacks were opened, the Judge saw in the first sack what appeared to be a human torso and legs; both were dark and showed signs of burning. The second sack contained a head and shoulders. They, too, were dark and burnt.

"Obviously, they cut the body into two parts and left both parts in the river with the hope of disposing of them permanently at a later time. But it so happened that the tide subsided, presenting the sacks to the flies," said E-Lung, wiping his hands.

Judge Quan now knew that he had the crucial evidence to reopen the murder case. He knew, also, that he was moving closer against Mrs Chu.

"Coroner Chen, I would like you and E-Lung to bring the body back to the Tribunal. Don't let it out of your sight. You may make all necessary preparations for another examination during the afternoon court session. I will pay a friendly visit to Candidate Soong."

As his two assistants left for the Tribunal, the Judge walked back to the hotel and ordered a Tribunal guard to call off the search. He jumped onto his horse and was about to gallop towards the Candidate's residence when suddenly he stopped and ordered the same guard to bring his official palanquin to the hotel. He would visit the Candidate in his full magisterial capacity.

Meanwhile, Candidate Soong sat impatiently in his home. He had been very concerned since he had received the letter from Judge Quan. What was the Judge up to? Was he here to arrest him or merely to pay him a friendly visit, as mentioned in the letter? Either way, it was extremely bad timing as he had already packed up most of his books and some of the furniture in the main lounge.

A servant came to indicate that the Judge was approaching. Candidate Soong hastily got up; brushed the new blue tunic he usually wore on official occasions, fixed his cap firmly on his head and walked to the entrance.

As the Judge's palanquin turned around the corner, Candidate Soong could see two Tribunal guards in their full armour on horseback, each carrying two large Tribunal banners that waved in the wind. Two other guards rode to the side and at the back of the palanquin. In all, it was an imposing and majestic sight. Candidate Soong was alarmed and took several deep breaths in order to collect himself.

When the palanquin finally stopped at the entrance, Judge Quan remained seated. Two guards dismounted and walked towards the Candidate, their long swords swinging through the air with every stride they made. One guard looked menacingly at him and announced in a loud voice that the Magistrate of Sui-chou had arrived. The Candidate and all the personnel of his household bowed respectfully to the Judge as he stepped from his palanquin.

Candidate Soong felt two strong hands grasping his shoulders as he slowly lifted his face and saw the Magistrate in his golden and black ceremonial clothes with the gold and black emblem of a dragon in the front. The bright afternoon sun shone from behind the Judge and his winged cap moved in the wind as he stared at the Candidate.

The Candidate suddenly took a step back, almost tripping over his servant. For a moment he thought he had seen the King of Darkness coming to take him to the underworld. Cold sweat flowed from his head as he righted himself once again. Then he wiped the sweat with his tunic sleeves and spoke in a low, nervous voice. "I am indeed honoured to have the Judge's company in my humble home."

Judge Quan smiled broadly, realizing that his plan to weaken Candidate Soong's resolve was working. "No, Candidate, given your family's reputation, the honour is mine!" he pronounced, inviting himself into the Soong residence.

In the courtyard the Judge paused and indicated to the Candidate that he should lead the way in.

The Candidate then took the Judge to the sparcly furnished family lounge. Perplexed, the Judge looked around and saw that the room was quite dusty. It seemed also that some furniture had been packed away in wooden boxes.

The Candidate invited the Judge to sit and ordered an assistant to bring some tea.

The Judge sat down with two guards by his side, continuing to survey the large, but almost empty room.

Before the Candidate could explain the unusual nature of the house, the Judge himself spoke. "Are you moving, Candidate?" he asked, in a matter-of-fact manner.

"Er...no, Your Honour." Candidate Soong found it difficult to answer the Judge and was able to muster enough courage to do so only after he had drunk the tea served for the Judge and himself.

"Only to the Capital, Quang Wu-meng!"

The Judge heard a strong clear voice from behind him. He felt a hand rest lightly on his shoulder. Annoyed at being addressed by his birth name, he swung around to see who the intruder was.

When Judge Quan saw who had spoken to him, he immediately fell onto his knees and prostrated himself in front of Soong Fu-Liu, father of Candidate Soong, primary adviser to the Emperor and the person who had given Judge Quan his current posting.

Elder Soong lifted the Judge with both arms and invited him to sit down, while he himself took the opposite chair. Candidate Soong remained standing behind his father.

Shaken by the sudden arrival of such an eminent person in his jurisdiction unannounced, the Judge was perplexed and momentarily lost for words. What had begun as a mission to shake Candidate Soong's resolve in the murder case had instead caught the Judge himself off his guard. Why was Elder Soong here in his town, at such a crucial moment of the murder investigation? Was it possible Elder Soong sought to intervene personally on his son's behalf?

"I make it a point to visit certain provinces unannounced, to judge for myself the state of affairs there. It is the only way I know to gain inside knowledge, before I give my advice to our illustrious Emperor."

"If you could have let me know of your planned arrival, I could have organized a more fitting welcome." But the Judge was cut short by Elder Soong. "That was exactly what I planned to avoid. It is better for me to see a province as it functions normally, rather than through a formal visit. I am indeed glad that you could pay the Soong residence a visit, Judge Quan Wu-meng. There is nothing so good as leaving the stifling walls of a

Tribunal and being out among the people you were placed to govern.

"I have heard from my son that you have done excellent work to resolve several cases already. In particular the murder case of the so-called Chu Fan-shing. You should really congratulate yourself. You have a strong deductive mind which should be the envy of most Judges. You have indeed exceeded all expectations of a magistrate in his inaugural position."

"I could not have done so without the help of my Sergeant and Constable. My predecessor also left the Jurisdiction in good order." Judge Quan looked at Candidate Soong when he mentioned the town's previous Judge. There was no reaction from the Candidate.

"In any case, it was excellent investigative work, Judge Quan. I have not acquainted myself with the full details, but I have heard something about it from my son and I was truly impressed." Elder Soong paused; looked at the bare room and than continued.

"My son could have learned much from your exemplary efforts, Judge Quan. But, I have decided to take him with me to the Capital. Since he has passed his local examination, I believe that he will now be able to advance himself further under my guidance and perhaps gain first-hand experience of the ins and outs of the Judiciary system.

Suspicious of Elder Soong's real intention, Judge Quan asked when he would be leaving for the Capital with his son. "It would be a great loss for this town if a reputed family such as the Soong left us," he said. "May I arrange a ceremony in which the whole town could be involved?"

Soong Fu-liu looked at his son and the Candidate nodded in agreement.

Elder Soong also agreed. "Of course, it would be the least we could do to repay the town for its hospitality. We intend to leave two days from today. The journey will be long, but the weather is good at this time of the year. It will also give me ample time to look around the province by myself."

"As magistrate, I must ask that, if there is anything that the Tribunal can do to assist you, please let me know. I shall be at your service."

After the Judge said this, he politely stood up, knelt down once more to the Elder, and bowed three times. He did not rise until the Elder lifted his shoulders to do so.

Candidate Soong then led the Judge out of the house and back to his palanquin.

As the procession wound its way back to the Tribunal, Judge Quan worried about the impact of Elder Soong's visit to the town on the murder case. In particular, he felt uneasy about Candidate Soong accompanying his father to the Capital, away from the Judge's grasp. Was Soong Fu-liu's visit aimed at protecting his son?

Soong Fu-liu's presence made it far more difficult to proceed with the case. It would be difficult to face up to a man so strong of will and so able in his knowledge of the Judiciary. Soong Fu-liu was not only the Emperor's adviser, but also a reformer of the current Judiciary system. The situation could well become one of a student standing up against his teacher.

Revenge from Beyond

Judge Quan Learns from the Old Hermit.

Judge Quan and Elder Soong Ride Behind E-Lung on their way to Mrs Chu's Residence. The Guild Master's Hotel is in the Background.

iii

CHAPTER FIFTEEN

*Throughout the murder investigation, the Judge had never
questioned who the perpetrator of the murder might be. As far as
the Judge was concerned, if that person was guilty of a crime,
then justice must be served against that person.*

The afternoon session ended with the beggar being taken
away to the Tribunal prison cell. Then both Coroner Chen
and E-Lung joined the Judge in the library. Coroner Chen looked
at the tired Judge and asked, "Your Honour, how did you know
the beggar was involved in the murder case?"

Judge Quan replied that he was, at first, surprised that this
beggar was the person he had seen underneath the archway two
days ago, brandishing his two sticks outside the town's hotel. But
this time he was without the distinctive chicken-feathered hat he
wore on that day. Who would have thought that this man would
be embroiled in this complicated murder case?

"Talking about the night before last, the Hotel Guild-Master
told me that the beggar suffered from a fever then, and in his
fever, kept asking for more rice, but when given it, pushed it
away. I found this curious. Perhaps the beggar was rambling and
not talking about rice at all! After all, the beggar was lying in a
hotel owned by the man who had had the Rice-merchant killed.
Was he talking about the merchant of rice, rather than rice itself?
I thought I would call him in for questioning on the slim chance
that he had some connection with the death of the Rice-
merchant. We now know that the beggar received a sum of
money from the Warden to help him switch bodies at the hotel.
On the next day when the beggar went to the hotel in town to
celebrate, he was involved in a brawl with a disgruntled
employee of the Guild-Master.

"Judging from the beggar's description of the employee's
behaviour, I wouldn't be surprised, Coroner, if he turned out to
be the employee who was your table-companion yesterday
morning at the tea-house."

The Judge then asked about the body that had been recovered.

E-Lung poured both Judge Quan and Coroner Chen some tea
while the Coroner explained that the Rice-merchant's body was
now guarded by four officers in the Tribunal's morgue. He went

on to explain that a preliminary examination of the Rice-merchant's throat confirmed that he had been killed before the hotel fire. Coroner Chen surmised that the murder case could now be reopened.

After Coroner Chen completed his report, he noticed that the Judge looked perturbed. Something was on the Judge's mind. Both Coroner Chen and E-Lung became worried when the Judge explained that Soong Fu-liu was in town and in two days time would leave for the Capital with his son.

"Soong Fu-liu is here? In town?" E-Lung asked. "What would Elder Soong be doing in our town in the middle of a murder investigation, especially when the Tribunal is weaving a tighter and tighter web around his son?"

"I asked myself that question on my way back from the Soong residence. I do not know the real purpose of Elder Soong's visit. The secrecy of his arrival was indeed unusual in the official sense, but totally understandable from a man who has often done the unexpected."

"I presume that Elder Soong didn't mention the murder case to Your Honour or ask Your Honour for his favourable consideration towards the case on behalf of his son?" Coroner Chen spoke half-heartedly as if he already knew the answer.

"Only that his son had told him about the Tribunal's excellent deductive capacity in resolving several difficult cases, including the Fan-shing murder case. He did not mention a favourable outcome. In fact Elder and Candidate Soong still believe that the Prefect will soon close the murder case.

Elder Soong said that his visit was strictly a fact-finding journey on behalf of the Emperor, that maintaining secrecy is his way of obtaining a true opinion of the provinces that he visits. But the difference here was that he would take his son back to the Capital after his visit. He mentioned that the Candidate had already passed the local examination and would now stand a better chance of advancing further under his father's tutorship in the Capital, as he continues to serve the Emperor."

"His son bribed the examiners to pass the local examination. Does Your Honour think Elder Soong knew about his son's involvement in the murder case?" E-Lung asked dryly.

"There was no reason why Elder Soong would be involved," Judge Quan replied. "He has only recently arrived in the town and furthermore, his reputation and position puts that question beyond any doubt."

Coroner Chen nodded his head in agreement.

Judge Quan appeared to focus on the inkwell on his desk. He toyed with the lion-shaped container, running his hands over the animal. – A small reservoir formed by the lion's mouth allowed the writer to quickly re-ink his brush.

Throughout the murder investigation, the Judge had never questioned who the perpetrator of the murder might be. As far as the Judge was concerned, if that person was guilty of a crime, then justice must then be served against that person. Only now did the Judge begin to consider that that person was the son of a powerful, able and experienced man. Nothing in the Judge's studies had prepared him for this situation. More importantly, Judge Quan felt that, with his very limited experience, he would not be able to move against a person like Elder Soong, who had an in-depth knowledge of the Empire's Judiciary system.

Knowing that the Judge was in no mood to discuss the case, Coroner Chen excused himself, and on behalf of E-Lung said that there was much to be done at the morgue. Both men then quietly left the library, leaving Judge Quan alone to decide on his next move.

Still toying with the ink-well, Judge Quan's thoughts slowly drifted to the old hermit and his surroundings. The coolness and calmness of the air within the cavern appeared before him to soothe his troubled mind. The Judge recollected the cavern, the old and unused scrolls, the meditation mat, the light, and finally the boiling cauldron. He then remembered the hermit's face, smooth and unwrinkled, like that of a young person, while his long white hair and beard appeared to reveal age.

Gradually, Judge Quan noticed that he was now able to fix his thoughts on the hermit's teachings. He tried to recollect the words that they had exchanged. First, a person's name was a fixed label placed on an ever-changing self. Second, suffering and difficulties were your friends, not your enemies, for it was only through such experiences that one would grow. Finally, holding onto old and unused teachings had little or no relevance to today.

Then, as if struck by lightning, Judge Quan opened his eyes to the present. He smiled to himself, rested his head on his arms on the library desk, and fell into a long and peaceful sleep.

CHAPTER SIXTEEN

*Through the course of my lifetime's work, I have made
innumerable enemies who would like nothing better
than to see me and my family fall.*

Judge Quan ascended the dais in his full ceremonial clothes
and took his seat behind the bench. Large crowds occupied
the courtroom for the morning session. Many of the townspeople
appeared to be in court, all of them expecting that the Tribunal
would continue the murder investigation into the Fan-shing case.

The Judge noted that Elder Soong was sitting at the back of
the courtroom, probably acting as an observer. He wore a
common blue tunic and a black cap, none of which suggested to
the people around him that they were in the presence of one of
the most eminent and powerful figures in the Empire.

The presence of Elder Soong did not surprise the Judge, but
the absence of Candidate Soong and Mrs Chu worried him. What
had the two lovers been up to since the unannounced arrival of
Candidate Soong's father?

Coroner Chen and E-Lung took their usual positions behind
the Judge. They both knew that the Tribunal had enough
evidence to bring the Warden out for questioning. They had also
observed the cowardly behaviour of the Warden in the Tribunal
prison cell and were sure that he would implicate Candidate
Soong and Mrs Chu with the application of minimal force. But
they had also seen the Judge's uncertain reaction to Elder
Soong's unexpected appearance in the town. Neither knew what
course of action, if any, the Judge would take.

Judge Quan rapped twice with the gavel to commence the
court session. He dealt, first, with the usual routine matters of the
court.

Then he announced in a loud voice for all to hear, "For the
past three days, this Tribunal has worked diligently on the Fan-
shing murder case. The Tribunal has uncovered cruel and sinister
activities intended to pervert the course of justice, as well as
blatant tampering of criminal evidence by certain individuals in
this town. To answer these charges, I now call the Warden of the
Western sector out for questioning."

The young Warden was dragged out to the court for the first time. He was clad in a gray loose tunic, bearing the stench of his prison cell. Both his hands were bound behind him. He bowed low as if to hide his face from the people in court and then a guard at his side forced him to kneel down before the Judge who sat imposingly in front of him.

Nothing in the Warden's life-experience had prepared him for this day. He had never before disobeyed the law and been paraded before so many people. He knew little about the judiciary system, having learned only what was required to perform his role as Warden. The sight of Judge Quan's deathly-still and frowning figure and the numerous torture implements clearly visible to him frightened the young and simple-minded man.

Elder Soong overheard people murmuring about the Fan-shing case. Thinking that there must have been some mistake as, to his knowledge, the case had been closed, he slowly worked his way towards the front. The people around him were at first annoyed as he pushed his way through them, but, when they saw who he was, they quickly made room, allowing him to move to the front of the courtroom.

Judge Quan avoided Elder Soong's bewildered stare and began to question the Warden.

"How long have you served as Warden of the Western sector?" Judge Quan asked in a soft and friendly voice.

"This... this... this insignificant person was appointed Warden not more then six months ago, Your Honour."

"And in your short time as Warden, you acted competently in your capacity. Is that not right?"

"I always thought of my appointment as the most fortunate event of my life. I never underestimated my position and always did my utmost to fulfill the responsibilities of my job as Warden."

"A privileged position such as yours must require a nomination from someone before you could finally be appointed. I would like to know who nominated you for Warden and who guided you in your learning and activities. You certainly performed your tasks well and you must have had a good teacher. Please let this court know the name of that teacher."

"For many years I had nothing but bad luck on my side. Without work or the means to gain a decent livelihood, I begged for my food out on the streets. One day however, a man saw me and took pity on me. He was kind enough to bring me to his residence; gave me food and treated me as his friend. For a while, I lived and worked in his household, until one day he spoke to me and asked if I would be interested in a job as Warden. I was surprised but accepted without any hesitation. I thought that my luck had changed for the better. Nothing in my whole life would have suggested to me that I might become a Warden. So, during my work in that role, I performed my tasks as diligently as I could."

"So," the Judge clarified, "You were living out on the streets and six months ago, this man – shall we say, your benefactor? – helped you into this position as Warden?"

"Yes!"

There were murmurs of disbelief in the courtroom. How could a beggar be picked from obscurity to be given such a privileged position, a position that any person in town would have been delighted to occupy, let alone someone from the streets? The people were incredulous that a beggar could have beaten all rivals for this appointment. There must have been some other purpose in it.

The Elder Soong realized that this Judge had uncovered yet another corrupt activity in the murder case. He observed the people's reaction around him; smiled at the Judge and guessed that this Magistrate would not relent until all questions in this murder case had been answered truthfully. He noted with satisfaction that this Judge would serve the Empire well.

"This was indeed an extremely unusual appointment, don't you think, Warden?" the Judge asked, after all the noise in the courtroom had subsided.

"Yes Your Honour, but I never questioned why I should have been appointed to this position. I just wanted to prove my worth to my benefactor and ensure that all my tasks were done thoroughly."

"Tell this court the name of the benefactor who treated you so well. This court would like to reward and recognize such good deeds," the Judge requested him, kindly.

"He is a good man Your Honour. I do not believe I did anything wrong in my capacity as Warden of the Western sector and as such I did not question the reputation of my benefactor...." The Warden tried to answer but was suddenly cut short by the Judge.

"You have been accused of perverting the course of justice and tampering with murder evidence. These are serious accusations against you and reflect back to your benefactor. If you do not want to mention his name, then look around the courtroom and answer whether he is here right now. If you do not, this court will give you fifty lashes for your hesitation." With these words, the Judge relinquished his previously friendly approach to the Warden.

A guard grabbed the Warden's arm and lifted him to his feet. Frightened by the Judge's sudden anger, the Warden slowly began to look round the courtroom. Judge Quan's eyes rested on Elder Soong who stared at the Judge encouragingly. The Judge then knew that Elder Soong knew little about the case and was never involved in it.

As the Warden ended his search and looked back at the Judge to shake his head, the guard forced the Warden to kneel on the ground again. "Speak up, Warden! Who is your benefactor?"

When there was no answer from the Warden, Judge Quan angrily took from the cylindrical holder to his right a sign with the words, "fifty lashes" written on it. Judge Quan then summarily threw the notice on to the floor, effectively giving the order for the beatings to begin.

Two guards dragged back further the struggling Warden's body, and forced him to face flat down onto the floor. The Warden's clothes were partially stripped off to reveal his buttocks as two other guards each grabbed hold of a long red bamboo batten in full view of the frightened Warden.

As the Judge had already given the order to begin the torture, the first guard began without haste. He lifted the long batten high above his head and brought it down onto the Warden's bare skin. As it struck, the force of the impact made a loud sound in the courtroom and a cry of agony from the Warden went in unison with the stroke. No sooner was the first stroke completed, than the next guard continued with the next. In this way, the accused had no time to recover from each stroke.

Sweat flowed freely from the Warden's forehead with each new stroke on his bare buttocks. After a time, his bare skin broke and blood could be seen slowly flowing from the welts that had formed. His loud and desperate screams were quickly replaced by long groans of agony as he began to slip into unconsciousness.

Racked by pain and anger at having been mistreated by life, the Warden lifted his head and looked at the Judge, but before he could open his mouth to speak, his head dropped, and his body went limp as he fainted from his ordeal.

Judge Quan ordered the proceedings to stop and sour tea was quickly administered to revive the Warden. Slowly, he regained consciousness and was helped back onto his knees. When he finally looked at the Judge, he was startled to see that his friend the beggar was also kneeling in front of the Judge, but at some distance to his left.

"State your name to this court. Have you ever met this man – this so-called Warden – before?" Judge Quan asked the beggar.

"I... I am a simple man who has lived in the streets all my life. I do not even know who gave birth to me. How am I to know what my name is? As to this Warden – yes I know him – we were friends back in the days when he also was on the street. Two days ago, he asked me to assist him and together we carried a heavy sack to the top floor of the hotel. He didn't tell me what was inside the sack. I was given some money for my trouble and left him alone inside the hotel room." The beggar completed his statement, all the while staring at the Warden.

Elder Soong looked at Judge Quan proudly, hoping that one day his son would be as strong and as shrewd as this Judge.

"This beggar has placed you in the same room as the burnt victim. What do you have to say to that? I don't truly believe that you acted alone. I know that you must have had other help. But whoever that person may be, he is not here in the court today to help you. You have been abandoned. You were used. Now, I ask you one last time, Warden. Who was your benefactor?"

Gradually, the Warden lifted his tired body to look at the Judge. Then he slowly moved his body to look at his beggar friend before finally facing Elder Soong. He then said, hesitatingly, "He was ... Master ... Candidate Soong."

The whole court fell into an uproar when they heard that a member of the Soong family had been implicated in the murder. Someone in the crowd asked his neighbour who else among the prominent people of the town was involved in this far-reaching murder case. Then they looked in the direction of Elder Soong.

The Primary Adviser was furious; he looked up angrily.

Before the loud commotion had subsided, Judge Quan once more spoke angrily. "You insolent pig, are you trying to put all the blame for your crimes on the Candidate? Do you not know that he is a renowned and reputed citizen of our town? How dare you bring such slanderous and false accusations against this man? Did you not demand more money from the Candidate? In fact, did you not dare to blackmail the Candidate for your own benefit?" The Judge pointed his large finger at the already frightened Warden.

Elder Soong stamped towards the front of the bench, effectively breaking courtroom protocol. He stood in front of the bench and looked up at the Judge. "Magistrate Quan," he said, "I demand that you punish this Warden for spreading lies about my son."

The whole courtroom became silent, no-one daring to speak, no-one wanting to disturb the two able and strong-minded law-enforcers suddenly pitched against each other. Coroner Chen looked at E-Lung worriedly.

Judge Quan paused for a moment and attempted to think of a way out of the situation he had effectively created by bringing out the Warden for questioning. It was clear to him that, in order to serve the people well, he must gain their confidence. He knew that if he was seen to back out, justice would not be served and the people would perceive his court as a convenient tool that the rich could manipulate, sending a wrong impression to the people of this town.

"Elder Soong," he said then, "You are a highly respected citizen of this town and your work is highly regarded throughout this glorious Empire. Rest assured, in light of this development, that I, as Magistrate, will consider most seriously these accusations against your son."

Judge Quan paused slightly and was interrupted by Elder Soong himself. "As a prominent person in this Empire," the Elder said, "I naturally advise the Emperor on policies which might not be agreeable to many. Through the course of my lifetime's work, I have made innumerable enemies who would like nothing better then to see me and my family fall. But to attack me through the exploitation of my innocent son is a cowardly and desperate act. I demand that the Judge punish this liar immediately and put an end to his slanderous words." Elder Soong stood firmly in front of the Judge, his fists clenched as he emphasized each word.

"Punish I will," Judge Quan replied clearly to the Elder, "But only in due course if the lies are substantiated. I therefore ask the Eminent Soong to let this Court continue its questions unhindered."

The incensed Elder Soong approached closer to the bench, again breaching the normal protocol of the courtroom. "Beware, Magistrate! I hold a higher office then you do. Though I am here merely on a visit to this region, I still hold the power to replace any local Magistrate whom I believe to be unfit and deem unable to conduct his role in a proper and just manner. Magistrate Quan, do not force me to use my reserved powers." Elder Soong spoke softly and clearly to the Judge, while at the same time staring fixedly at him to emphasise his point.

Judge Quan took this as a direct threat, knowing that Elder Soong indeed had authority over him. It was, however, clear in the Judge's mind that the people must be aware of the developments that had been uncovered and also under what circumstances he could be replaced as the local magistrate. He stood up from his chair, looked away from Elder Soong and spoke directly and with conviction to the people.

"I, Magistrate Quan, have for the past few days diligently investigated the Fan-shing murder case. Although, at first, this court recommended that the Prefect should close the case, it has reversed its decision after discovering a third murdered body and hearing the Warden's accusation of Candidate Soong. Candidate Soong now stands accused, but his father, the Eminent Soong Fu-liu, has today stood against this Court and has threatened to replace the Magistrate with himself. I suggest that a father cannot, in an unbiased way, preside over a case in which his son stands accused, for whatever reason."

When the Judge had finished, he looked straight at Elder Soong, making clear his intention to continue with the case.

Elder Soong shook his head in utter disbelief at the Judge's intention to carry on a course of action that would destroy the reputation of the Soong family and bring down his only son. He also knew that the Judge's speech effectively questioned the appropriateness of his replacing the Judge and presiding over a case in which he might be a direct beneficiary.

Elder Soong then turned around and faced the people in the courtroom. "I am a citizen of this town," he declared, "And I therefore have a vested interest, especially when, in my opinion, this Judge is determined to continue a process which I believe may be detrimental to certain citizens. This issue must be resolved in private without any delay."

Elder Soong turned round and faced Judge Quan. This time, however, both Coroner Chen and E-Lung stepped forward to show their support for their Judge. Unperturbed, Elder Soong continued to speak to the Judge and to the court. "This morning's court session is adjourned, so that I, Soong Fu-liu, Primary Adviser to the August Emperor, may consider whether this Judge is of sound mind and whether he is fit to proceed with the demanding and arduous role of a Magistrate."

Judge Quan then had no choice but to rap the gavel once, turn around and walk out of the Tribunal. Coroner Chen and E-Lung were about to follow but Elder Soong ascended the dais, stood in their path and gave them a sharp and angry look before leaving the courtroom and following the Judge.

Coroner Chen and E-Lung looked at each other and then at the crowded courtroom. Unable to support and protect their Judge, the two men and the people wondered who would preside over the deepening and far-reaching criminal investigation and who next would govern the people of the town.

CHAPTER SEVENTEEN

This journey on behalf of the Emperor had turned out to be a homecoming trip in which he would be reunited with his son. He patted him and assured him that all would be fine; that the truth would come out and that the Soong name would be cleared.

"Magistrate Quan, it is obvious to me that you are intent on a course of action to destroy my family's reputation. I seriously doubt that that insolent Warden spoke the truth. Why do you appear to believe those lies? Do you not know I have many enemies throughout this Empire?" Elder Soong stood facing the Judge, speaking strongly and with his right hand clenched into a fist.

Cold air flowed from the Tribunal library window as the Judge invited Elder Soong to sit in the visitor's chair. He then closed the wooden framed window and sat behind his library desk.

"From my very first day, you have looked upon me favourably and I must express my deepest gratitude to you for my appointment to this post as local magistrate. I ask you to continue your confidence in me and allow me to continue presiding over this case. You said that you would like your son to return to the Capital for his own good. But if you preside over this case and if it were to close prematurely, rumours would spread in the Capital. Your son's and your family's name will forever be tainted unless we are able to arrive at the truth."

There was a long silence in the library as Judge Quan allowed Elder Soong to consider the situation. Judge Quan had repeated his point more than enough. He knew that neither of them would relent. Elder Soong had too much pride to allow the name of Soong to be mentioned in the Tribunal records in relation to any criminal or bad deeds whereas, as local magistrate, it was up to him, Quan, to take what he believed to be the proper course of action. The rest would be up to Elder Soong. It was he who must resolve this stalemate.

"Magistrate Quan!" Elder Soong was the first to break the silence, looking straight at the Judge. "I cannot let you preside over this case. I see my enemies at work here. I know too much about the court's matters at the Capital, I know where my enemies come from and I know which cases they object to. I am sorry but this case is too large for a local magistrate. I will make a note to the Prefect that I am replacing you as Judge only temporarily, not because of your lack of ability; but because of my in-depth knowledge of those against me. I am the best person to preside over this case, Magistrate Quan. I now ask you to hand me the seal of office immediately." Elder Soong finished speaking and raised both his hands as if to receive the seal.

Judge Quan rose from his chair and stared at Elder Soong. For a moment, the Elder thought the Judge wished to dispute the transfer of the office seal. But when he was about to repeat his demand, Quan walked over to his left where a series of wooden lattices acted as book-shelves. A large rectangular box could be seen on the top shelf. It was wrapped in a red cloth and tied with a large knot.

Judge Quan reverently brought the seal down from the shelf with both hands. He then slowly carried the seal above his head towards Elder Soong. The Elder Soong stood up, ready to accept the seal and with it the responsibility of governing the town.

When Judge Quan approached the Elder, he sank to his knees and bowed. Elder Soong paused for a moment and was reaching out his hands to accept the seal, when suddenly there was a knock at the door.

A determined E-Lung stepped into the library and saw Judge Quan on his knees. He himself quickly knelt down apologetically and explained why he had abruptly intruded the proceedings. "Your Honour!" E-Lung said, looking from one to the other of the two men, wondering to whom he should report. "Candidate Soong is missing!"

Judge Quan looked up at the Elder. Seeing the Elder's bewildered look, he looked back at E-Lung and asked, "Where is Mrs Chu?"

"We have received no word from the guards we placed there," E-Lung replied. "I suspect she is still at her residence."

"E-Lung," Judge Quan replied with decision, "We have no time to lose. Arrange horses for us all, including Elder Soong. In fact, show Elder Soong to his horse now. We must leave immediately. I will explain everything along the way." Judge Quan looked at the Elder as he stood up.

Not really knowing what the commotion was about, Elder Soong followed E-Lung. Judge Quan immediately placed the seal back on the shelf and headed for the Tribunal entrance.

Outside the Tribunal, the sun had already risen high above in the sky but the air was still cool and refreshing. But Judge Quan had no time to appreciate the weather. He saw that two horses had been harnessed by E-Lung and that Elder Soong was already mounted. Judge Quan quickly straddled his horse and led the way towards Mrs Chu's residence.

Before long they reached the bridge overlooking the Guild-Master's hotel. Judge Quan slowed down so that both E-Lung and Elder Soong could catch up with him. Riding side-by-side with Elder Soong, Judge Quan told him that his son had been having an affair with Mrs Chu and that both had conspired with the Warden to murder Fan-shing. Elder Soong was unbelieving and aghast but before he could protest and repudiate what he heard, Judge Quan rode forward and led the three men towards Mrs Chu's residence.

Once outside the residence, E-Lung headed towards two men standing near to the house. Disguised as beggars, both men were eating from bowls of noodles while keeping a close watch on Mrs Chu's residence. When they saw E-Lung, they immediately stopped eating, stood up and joined their commander. They reported to E-Lung that no-one had left the house, at least while they were watching it. E-Lung returned to the Judge and asked permission to enter the Chu residence. Judge Quan nodded and remained standing with the two guards as E-Lung quickly disappeared down a back alley-way.

While E-Lung was gone, Judge Quan advised Elder Soong of the importance of following this investigation through. If his son was indeed found within the confines of Mrs Chu's residence, then it would raise serious questions about his relationship with Mrs Chu and whether they were both involved in the murder of Mrs Chu's husband.

When E-Lung reached the rear of Mrs Chu's residence, he looked for two other guards who had been placed there to keep a watch. They were nowhere to be seen, and E-Lung swore that he would discipline both men for their sloth. Their lack of attention could jeopardize the case.

Revenge from Beyond

E-Lung looked round to make sure that no-one was watching him and than quickly hoisted himself over the wall into Mrs Chu's yard. This was the first time that E-Lung had entered the Chu residence, but from Coroner Chen and the Judge's description, he was able to head straight for the window next to the rear entrance of the house. As he peered through the partially opened window and saw that no-one was there, he heard noises upstairs and immediately headed for the boundary wall between the Chus' and their neighbours' residence.

As E-Lung ran towards the wall, he felt a hand on his shoulder. He immediately turned in an attempt to deflect it. He was about to strike his attacker when he suddenly realized that the hand belonged to one of the two guards who now stood right behind him. This was not an appropriate time to discipline them. Instead E-Lung instructed them to break into the rear entrance on his signal, after he had climbed onto the neighbour's roof.

He climbed skilfully onto the boundary wall and then onto the roof, careful not to make the same mistake as Judge Quan who had slipped and fallen onto the wooden crates below. He could still see the broken crates that had cushioned the Judge's fall.

Crouching on the wall, E-Lung could hear noises coming from Mrs Chu's bedroom. He peered through the window and could just see a male and a female sitting on the bed. The man had his right arm around the female. The sound was muffled but E-Lung heard him mention the Capital and how they would be free there from the attentions of the local Judge. E-Lung looked carefully at the room and when he thought that it was safe to proceed, he covered his head with his arms and jumped through the window. As the fragile wooden and paper material of the window fragmented, Mrs Chu jumped off the bed and headed straight for the bedroom door. Candidate Soong wasn't so lucky. E-Lung managed to grasp his long loose sleeve, causing him to try desperately to free himself before being brought down. He collapsed onto the floor with E-Lung on top of him.

While maintaining a firm hold on his captive, E-Lung quickly got to his feet and pulled the Candidate up with him. The man attempted to struggle to break free but E-Lung delivered a hard blow to the Candidate's stomach, causing the man to lower his head towards the floor in agony, while at the same time E-Lung

129

lifted his fist to deliver a less severe blow to the Candidate's head. It was enough to startle and stop the Candidate from struggling any further.

Once he had subdued the Candidate, E-Lung needed only to hold onto the Candidate's right hand with his palm high above his back. Candidate Soong knew that if he continued to struggle, E-Lung would simply lift his arm higher above his back.

With his opponent subdued, E-Lung pushed him out of the bedroom and was immediately met by the two guards who had captured Mrs Chu. The three men then marched Mrs Chu and the Candidate through the front entrance of the house.

When Judge Quan and Elder Soong saw that the front gate to the Chu residence was open, they both approached it and were met first by Mrs Chu and then by Candidate Soong. When Elder Soong saw his son, he frowned in disbelief. For what reason would his son privately visit a widow?

One of the guards was about to tie Candidate Soong's hands behind his back, when Judge Quan stopped him. They would all ride back to town together, but Judge Quan did not want to bring the Soongs into further disrepute.

Elder Soong thought of giving his son a lecture but refrained from doing so in front of the Judge. He simply looked away from his son and rode back to the Tribunal alongside his colleague. Speechless, he knew that he had been away from his son far too long.

As the procession reached the town centre, a large curious crowd gathered. When they saw the four guards, two each at the front and two at the rear, they knew immediately that there had been another development in the ongoing murder case. The solemn face of Elder Soong and the frightened looks of Candidate Soong told the whole story, or at least some of it.

Once at the Tribunal, Mrs Chu was taken straight to a prison cell, while Candidate Soong was brought into the Tribunal library. Judge Quan left the father and son alone and joined his two loyal assistants.

"How did Your Honour know that the Candidate would be at Mrs Chu's residence?" E-Lung asked, looking at the Judge.

"I did not know for sure, but it was the first thought that came into my mind. I must congratulate you, E-Lung. Your timing was perfect. I was about to hand over the seal of office to Elder

Soong, when you suddenly came into the library." The Judge smiled once more and shook E-Lung's hand.

"What made Your Honour decide to pursue the Candidate when his father was in town?" Coroner Chen asked.

"While I was alone at the Tribunal library yesterday, I remembered the time that I had spent with the hermit. I couldn't quite understand all his teachings then, but suddenly everything fell into place. I understood for the first time what the hermit had said about a name being a label attached to an impermanent self. I feared Elder Soong's name and his reputation, knowing that he had helped to reform the Empire's judiciary. But I observed that he was willing to go against his own convictions when a member of his immediate family had fallen foul of the law. I saw Elder Soong as impermanent and rightly so, for he interpreted the law in his own way to protect his son, I saw in him then a weakness which I knew I could defeat.

I knew it would be difficult, but that if I did what I thought was right for the people and the law we would eventually get to the truth. This was another of the hermit's teachings. Also, when I looked at the lion-shaped ink-well in the palm of my hand and thought of the strength and majesty of a lion, I seemed to find the strength to pursue Candidate Soong in the presence of his father."

"Indeed, a supreme and sublime lesson from our Revered Judge Quan." Coroner Chen spoke somewhat impudently, and lowered his head to the Judge.

Then he and E-Lung broke out into loud laughter and the Judge, too, began to laugh. But when he turned to look at the closed library door, his smile was replaced by a solemn expression, reflecting a feeling of sorrow for the Soongs.

Although Elder Soong and his son sat next to each other in the library – a mere arm's length from each other – the distance between father and son had never been greater. Elder Soong thought again that perhaps he had left his son alone for far too long. He had hoped that the young man would develop into a respected man of literature in this quiet and faraway town, away from the disruptive and often addictive activities of the Capital. But being away from his son had also meant that he had not had the opportunity to spend time with him and guide his son's learning.

"They told me that Mrs Chu's husband was murdered, did you know anything about it?" Elder Soong asked, while looking at the painting behind the Judge's library desk.

Candidate Soong turned towards his father and knelt in front of him. Tearfully he looked at his father and shook his head in response. "I wanted to comfort her. That was all. We developed a good friendship after I first met her at the Guild-Master's hotel. I knew that she and her husband were quite poor, despite their expertise in their respective arts. I often lent them a hand in terms of money and in many ways I was their benefactor. When I heard Mrs Chu was grieving more and more about her husband's death, I felt compelled to see her and comfort her." Candidate Soong tearfully looked up at his father's eyes.

Elder Soong was surprised. He did not know whether to believe and feel proud of his son's acts of kindness or to decide that his son was once more trying to hide the truth from him.

"The Warden said it was you who promoted him from being a simple beggar to the post of Warden. Why would he say such things?" Elder Soong asked, looking down at his son.

"That's the truth. I took pity on him initially and gave him work around our house. When I saw how diligently he performed his tasks, I recommended him to the Judge of the day for the Warden's position. As far as I know, he performed his role well and there were no complaints from the people."

Candidate Soong suddenly stood up and reached for his father, crying loudly that he had tried to do good for the people of the town but in the process had never anticipated that the family's name would be ruined by his careless actions. He continued to cry like a child on his father's shoulder.

Elder Soong grasped his son in kindly fashion. Affected by his son's grief, he felt reassured by his explanations. This journey on behalf of the Emperor had turned out to be a homecoming trip in which he would be reunited with his son. He patted him and assured him that all would be fine; that the truth would come out and the Soong name would be cleared.

Candidate Soong knelt again and bowed profusely. He now knew that his father would intervene on his behalf.

There was a knock at the library door and Judge Quan, his two assistants and two other guards stepped in. Before he could be escorted away, Candidate Soong wiped his tears from his eyes; turned to look at his father and was reassured. The Elder Soong looked at the Magistrate and said, "Magistrate Quan you have been right all along. I am emotionally involved in this case. You are the best person to get at the truth and clear the name of the Soongs. I am sure that you will find my son to be innocent. His life and that of mine are in your capable hands."

"You, Candidate! How did you get into Mrs Chu's residence without being noticed?" E-Lung asked roughly, as Candidate Soong walked in front of him. The Candidate quickly turned to E-Lung and stared at him agitatedly. Elder Soong momentarily saw his son's reaction and suddenly sensed that he had understood his son wrongly.

CHAPTER EIGHTEEN

It appears that an attempt was made to conceal the stab wounds
by severing the body
in that exact same region.

Judge Quan ascended the dais and presided over the afternoon court session. He noticed Elder Soong sitting next to a guard at the front row. The Elder looked somewhat distant and dejected.

Judge Quan rapped the gavel twice and ordered the Warden to be brought into court. When the Warden was eventually brought out of his cell, he looked tired and his walk was almost lifeless. His hair was bound crudely and his tunic was moist with sweat. It was as if the Warden was on the brink and the Judge knew that he would talk without any resistance.

"This morning you confessed to this Court that you were a beggar from the streets but elevated to the role of Warden by the help of your benefactor, namely Candidate Soong. Is this correct?" Judge Quan asked the Warden loudly.

When the Warden quietly nodded his head to confirm, Judge Quan immediately spoke in a thunderous voice.

"Speak up, Warden!"

"That is true!" was the quick reply from the Warden.

"You may continue with your confession and I warn you, speak the truth. This Tribunal has not completed your fifty lashes. Now speak!"

The Warden was close to tears, feeling that he had to suffer this torture and humiliation all alone, while Candidate Soong and Mrs Chu were still free. The Warden then proceeded to confess his crime in full, not knowing that the court already had the two lovers in custody.

"I...I only did what I was told. Candidate Soong would give me orders. I felt compelled to obey them, because the Candidate had done so much for me and no-one else in this town had ever treated me as well as he did. Whatever the Candidate ordered, I would do it. I never feared being caught because the Candidate could always manage to encourage your predecessor's Tribunal to overlook our activities."

"Did you kill Fan-shing?" the Judge asked impatiently.

"I did!" There was a buzz in the courtroom. Those present were clearly united in their condemnation of the Warden. Finally, the murderer has been found, thought the Judge. He brought the courtroom back to order, and the Warden continued his confession.

"When I was told how to carry out the murder by Candidate Soong, I went to the Chu house and used a blow-pipe filled with poison. I inserted the pipe into a hole in the wall of the Chus' bedroom. It was arranged that Mrs Chu would give me a signal of three knocks on the wall when it was time to proceed. Once Fan-shing was dead, the plan was to kill someone else and make it look as though that person had murdered Fan-shing. He, in turn, would die and that would bring an abrupt end to the murder case."

"Why the Rice-merchant? How did you kill him?" Judge Quan asked the Warden, looking at Elder Soong, who appeared oblivious of the court's proceedings. Judge Quan stared at the Warden, knowing that he had so far spoken the truth, in particular about the blow-pipe. For this was consistent with what the Coroner had previously discovered.

"I think that Fan-shing must have lost a considerable amount of money during one of his gambling bouts. All I knew was that, on the day of his death, we were to wait for the Rice-merchant at Mrs Chu's house to collect Fan Shing's paintings. "Then Mrs Chu offered the Merchant some tea into which we had previously mixed a drug. Once the Rice-merchant was unconscious, I stabbed him several times with a knife and stuffed the body and the blood-soaked sheet into a rice bag.

"It was nightfall before I proceeded towards the hotel where I paid the beggar to help me move the rice sack to the Merchant's room. Once there, I quickly shifted the Merchant's body into a sitting position at a table and began to boil some water on the tea-stove, hoping that this would eventually set the hotel and the Rice-merchant on fire. I then casually walked down the stairs and headed for the hotel lockers.

"No one was around to notice me. Everyone was either in the tea-house or the gambling-room, so I was free to move within the hotel. I had previously befriended a disgruntled employee of the hotel who, after many cups of wine, told me how to operate the lockers. It therefore took very little time to plant the two paintings by Fan-shing in them. This would then allow Mrs Chu to declare these paintings as lost.

"That night, from outside the Rice-merchant's room," the Warden continued, "I saw Your Honour looking inside the Rice-merchant's mouth. I sensed that there was a problem, so I went to see the Candidate who was hiding near the river. I told him about my worries. Once more, the Candidate had the answers and gave orders for me to replace the Rice-merchant's body with another, namely that of Examiner Shao. I was then to dispose of the Rice-merchant's body in the river.

"Being a Warden, I had easy access to the Rice-merchant's body. With time on my side, I went to Examiner Shao's home and easily subdued the old man by a hard blow to his head. He was unconscious, but alive. As the night began to fall, I quickly disguised myself as a refuse-collector. I was used to the smell, having previously being a beggar. During the night, I bundled the unconscious body into a rice bag and carried him on a cart that was full of the town's refuse. The guard at the Western Gate let me through immediately, not wanting to smell the contents of my cart. I then headed for the mountains and away from the town, under the guiding light of the moon.

Once I came to a suitable spot, I bound the Examiner's hands and legs so that he could not escape; positioned his body against two rocks as if he was sitting down, then covered it with firewood and proceeded to set it and the body alight. The old Examiner Shao struggled weakly, but his struggle was in vain.

On the journey back, the guard once more let me through without any search. When I reached the hotel, I saw the Tribunal guard posted outside the Rice-merchant's room. He was asleep. I told him that if the Magistrate found out he would be in grave trouble. So I proposed to him that he should go for a meal at the hotel tea-house while I myself guarded the crime scene. It was then that my beggar friend helped me to carry the rice sack to the room, where I quickly switched the bodies and even had enough time to dispose of the Rice-merchant's body. All this was done before the Coroner was able to examine the body."

The Warden completed his confession with his head bowed. The Tribunal scribe read it back to him and the Warden in turn placed his thumb mark on the confession.

"Let it be known," Judge Quan announced, "that the Rice-merchant's body was switched before the Coroner could conduct his examination. In fact, the Tribunal looked at the wrong body, namely that of the Examiner, who had previously been killed by the Warden while still unconscious. However, this Tribunal has managed to recover the real Rice-merchant's body from the river at exactly the location mentioned by the Warden. I now ask the Coroner to examine this body for the Tribunal."

The Rice-merchant's body was taken out of the sack. It had been cut in two. Both parts were obviously charred from a fire and were stone hard.

Coroner Chen took some time to examine the exterior of the body. In particular, he paid special attention to the severed section.

"This victim is a middle-aged male. His upper body has been severed around the waist, possibly by an axe. It seems that he was killed by multiple stab wounds around the stomach." The Coroner suddenly paused and moved his head for a closer examination.

"It appears that an attempt was made to conceal the stab wounds by severing the body in that exact same region. The point of entry of the stab wounds can't be seen due to the extensive deterioration of the outer skin by the fire but, by looking at the cross section of the body, I can see clearly the several marks of the knife that entered the victim's stomach. Your Honour, this man died a slow, bleeding death."

With the Judge's approval, Coroner Chen then began to examine the victim's throat. He repeated exactly the same procedure as before and managed to extract a specimen. This was put into a bowl and brought to the Judge who took a close look and smiled. The bowl was then taken around the court for all to see. The Coroner continued with his report.

"Your Honour, the places where the body was cut in two show no signs of burning. Together with the concealed stab-wounds, the entry-point indicates a sequence of events. It appears that the stab-wounds killed the victim. – It is possible to see the knife entry-points on the skin. – After the stabbing, the body was burnt. This made the outer body unrecognizable and concealed the entry-point of the knife. After that the body was cut in two. That explains why the internal organs around the cross section of the body were not charred."

The Coroner listened carefully to the scribe who read aloud the Coroner's findings. He then nodded his agreement and stamped his seal onto the report.

The Magistrate thanked the Coroner and, ignoring the excited murmurs in court, said, "The Warden's extraordinary confession and the Coroner's findings have proved to this court that there was a sinister plan to murder certain individuals. In the light of these findings and numerous questions as yet unanswered, this Tribunal cannot in conscience let this murder case remain closed. I hereby pronounce the Fan-shing murder case reopened." Judge Quan completed his announcement with two raps of the gavel to emphasize his point to the people.

A loud cheer erupted in the court, supporting the Judge's strong stance on justice.

When the courtroom became silent once more, Judge Quan continued. "I now call upon Candidate Soong to appear before this court for questioning in relation to the case!"

As if suddenly awakened, Elder Soong turned his attention to the Judge, uncertain what his son would say during the forthcoming session.

CHAPTER NINETEEN

You will always be my son. Forgive me for all the wrongs I have done you; but I am afraid that you have erred in very many ways.

"It wasn't me. I didn't do it!" The scream came from Candidate Soong as he was unceremoniously dragged to face the bench. He struggled hard to break free, but then he saw the Warden kneeling down in front of the Judge with his head bowed; and the Candidate suddenly yelled at him in anger.

"What have you done to me, you good-for-nothing, dumb beggar? If it weren't for me, you would still be out on the streets. Damn you, damn you," the Candidate screamed at the Warden but was prevented from reaching him by a Tribunal guard. When he looked around and saw the silent figure of his father in the front row, the Candidate immediately fell silent.

"Candidate Soong, you are implicated in the murder of three persons, the artist Chu Fan-shing, the Rice-merchant and Examiner Shao. If you think you are innocent, speak the truth; prove to this court that you are free from any wrong-doings and do not attempt to hide behind your rage and anger."

"I had nothing to do with any murder, and certainly had no involvement with this fool in any of his disgusting crimes."

Judge Quan wondered at the unusual behaviour of the Candidate. If he were innocent, would he not be more composed, especially in the presence of his father?

"Warden!" Judge Quan shouted, and the Warden lifted his head. "Is this the man you mentioned as your benefactor and who you said gave the orders and the methods for killing the three men?"

The Warden looked at the Candidate and than lowered his head and nodded in agreement.

"Your Honour," wailed the Candidate, "it is the beggar's words against mine."

"This Tribunal would prefer to believe you, but you must answer all its questions truthfully. Where were you two nights ago?" the Judge asked.

"I was studying, Your Honour!"

"Yet my Sergeant saw you and this Warden at Mrs Chu's residence. Speak the truth, Candidate!"

"The Soong family has many enemies who are willing to spread lies in return for money."

"So, both the Warden and my Sergeant are liars? Then where were you three nights ago?"

"I am a studious person Your Honour. I may have passed my local...."

The Judge interrupted him by slamming his hand against the bench. "I myself heard you and Mrs Chu that night at her home. Are you accusing me and therefore this Tribunal of lying?"

Elder Soong sensed his son had not spoken the truth and that he was hiding certain facts from the court. He rose from his chair; approached the Candidate and spoke softly to him, a lone voice in a deathly silent courtroom.

"My son, you are all I have, I will always love you and think about you. If you believe that there was a conspiracy against our name, then speak the truth. Do not bend it but defend the truth. I will always be on your side, my son. Always."

Candidate Soong looked up at his father and suddenly his face turned red with rage. He swung round and would have reached his father had he not been pinned down by two of the Tribunal's guards. He began to spit at his father while at the same time tears flowed freely down his face.

"You're not my father! You never were and never will be!" The Candidate looked at Elder Soong who remained standing.

"He is your son. Your real son, I am nothing to you." The Candidate pointed at the Judge. "I hate you. I have hated you ever since my mother died. You never came to me. Instead you just concentrated on your work. I was no-one to you, so don't call me your son. You constantly scolded me and told me what was right and wrong. But they were never *my* rights and wrongs; they were always yours. Whenever I did the right thing, people would compare me to you, saying that Elder Soong would have done better. Why me? You want me to tell the truth? You want me to defend the truth? So here it is. Listen, Father and for once you may learn something from your son."

Candidate Soong quickly turned towards the Judge and continued his speech. It was as if all those years of hate and anger now began to pour out of the Candidate.

"When my mother died, I became a recluse without my father, until an old tutor was appointed for my care. He was old, yet in many ways he was like a real father to me. He never scolded me and he taught me about literature in a way that my father couldn't.

"It wasn't long before I began to meet more people. As time went by and after the death of my tutor, I realized that the Soong name could really be a good thing, rather then something bad. I found that through my name I could often have my own way. I began to establish various connections in the judiciary system. I mixed with people in high positions. I could get my own way in business and I could be the person I wanted to be. Finally, after all those years of living in my father's shadow, I could be his equal or even better then he was.

"You see there were many people who wanted the Soong name for their own self-promotion. By having me in their presence during a banquet, I was effectively adding the name of Soong to their businesses. I made many friends and a lot of money that way.

"Then I realized that I could be even better than my father. I could extend my influence if I was part of the Judiciary system. What a wonderful irony! I would use the very system my father had built for my own gain. I decided to sit for the local examination. But I needed help. You see I never really liked to read or study. In fact I must admit I have never been as studious as my father is. So I solicited help from Your Honour's predecessor and several other examiners and I passed the exam.

"Then I met Mrs Chu at her husband's gallery. She was beautiful, elegant, graceful and very intelligent. She was everything I could wish for in life. To our surprise we both fell in love during one of her performances at the Guild-Master's hotel.

"She cared like no other. She loved me like my mother and it was the love I had always yearned for but which had been denied since I was a child. I had finally found someone who understood and loved me. I was not going to let her go out of my life, just as my mother and my tutor had slipped away from me.

"I don't know how it happened but, one day, she came to me, crying. She said that Fan-shing had somehow discovered our affair. He knew how I had passed my exam and he had threatened to report us to the Tribunal. I knew we could escape the charges as we were close friends of your predecessor, but when news came that a new Judge had been appointed to the town, Mrs Chu and I had to act quickly against Fan-shing, else we could never be together.

"Mrs Chu thought of a plan to get rid of her husband so that we could live together elsewhere. Just when my life was turning my way, this man, Fan-shing, was going to destroy everything I had worked towards. I could never allow that and so I agreed to her plan.

"It was all set in motion when I took a beggar from the street and used my influence with the previous Judge to grant the beggar the position of Warden. He would do all the work for us. Mrs Chu and I would remain in the background. In time we could bring a false accusation against him. He would then be disposed of easily and Mrs Chu and I could live together.

"By the time of Your Honour's arrival, the plan had already begun in earnest. We felt confident that we could still beat the law, especially when Your Honour was still adjusting to his new town and environment."

The Candidate's gaze moved away from the Judge and he stared at his father. "Are you listening to me, Father? For I have told the truth."

With tears in his eyes Elder Soong stood up and spoke to the Candidate: "You will always be my son. Forgive me for all the wrongs that I have done you; but I am afraid that you have erred in very many ways."

Elder Soong turned and slumped back onto his seat. It was as if a high-flying dragon had suddenly grown old and – unable to fly – had fallen straight down to the ground. Elder Soong sat there gazing in front of him, oblivious of what the Judge did to close this eventful session of the afternoon court.

CHAPTER TWENTY

*Tomorrow, he would bring Fan-shing back from the dead
and let him confront Mrs Chu.*

Judge Quan awoke from an uneasy sleep. This was the first time he had actually slept in his room. As he struggled awake, the developments in court from the previous day and the forthcoming questioning of Mrs Chu occupied much of his mind.

Immediately after the afternoon court session the previous day, the Judge and his two assistants had gathered in the Tribunal library to discuss developments. They were elated that this complicated and arduous murder case had finally come before the Tribunal. They discussed ways to curb Mrs Chu's speech and theatrics when they next questioned her in court and all three agreed that calm and persistent questioning was the best strategy to follow.

Although he was happy that the end of the case was near, the Judge felt something that he could not fully explain to himself. The challenges of the past few days had taken him away from the formalities of the court and left him with a sense of sadness and regret that there were certain people in society who would stop at nothing to get what they wanted.

He felt some sympathy for Elder Soong. At the end of the previous day's court session, the man had left abruptly. Guards had been sent to the Soong's residence and around the town, but he was nowhere to be found. Judge Quan feared for his safety.

When the morning court was about to begin, Judge Quan sat as usual behind the bench and looked down at his court. Once again it was filled with people who were curious about the new developments and what the Tribunal's next step would be.

The Judge looked at the guards, all standing erect in full armour. Then he rapped the gavel twice before announcing the opening of the morning's court session. "This Tribunal of the people has, in the past few days, overcome many obstacles in the investigation of Mr Fan-shing's murder. It is the Court's view that both the Rice-merchant and Examiner Shao were killed by the Warden to divert attention from the real cause of Fan-shing's murder. The Warden acted on orders given by Candidate Soong, while Soong himself acted in conjunction with his paramour,

Mrs Chu. It is this Court's opinion that Mrs Chu was the main instigator of these hideous and desperate crimes."

Judge Quan ordered a guard to bring Mrs Chu before the court. Her hands were tied behind her back. Despite her tangled hair, she was still an attractive woman. She had done away with her white mourning clothes and was now wearing a white tunic with intricate red patterns on the edge of her collar. Her hair was held together by the red hairpin she had worn during her first court appearance in which she had reported the death of her husband.

Judge Quan was satisfied that Mrs Chu did not know that the Tribunal had been active in her husband's case even though the Judge had officially closed it. Perhaps she thought she had been cleared of any wrong-doing and therefore no longer needed to be seen as the grief-stricken widow she had so effectively portrayed over the past few days. At least, the Judge thought, her surprise arrest would shock her into submission to the Court.

On the other hand, Mrs Chu was full of anger and outrage. Her unceremonious arrest yesterday, so soon after the closure of her husband's case, had left her very bitter. She, too, had thought long and hard how she would react in court when questioned. She knew her arrest meant the Court had insurmountable evidence against her. Furthermore, without her mourning clothes, she would give the wrong signal to the people in court, contradicting her former posturing as a grief-stricken wife. Her only way out would be to defy the Judge, in an attempt to persuade the people in the court to take her side.

"Mrs Chu, do you know why you are here today in this court?"

"This insignificant person was about to provide a proper burial for my husband when I was wrongly arrested and locked overnight in a dirty prison cell. I ask the Court and the people how can my husband ever be buried in peace, especially when his widowed wife is being hounded remorselessly by this Court?"

"Nonsense," Judge Quan said immediately. "From the manner in which you are dressed, one wonders whether you are providing for a burial or are about to go out for an evening banquet."

"My husband's burial requires more money than I now have. I must therefore break from normal tradition and dress for a final performance at the Guild-Master's hotel," Mrs Chu said, tears now beginning to appear in her eyes.

"You cannot expect this Court to believe your lies. The Court would willingly have provided you with a loan which you could easily have repaid from the sale of your residence. Also, if the hotel had not been set on fire, the Guild-Master would have welcomed your performance. Mrs Chu you are in contempt. Guards! Give her thirty strokes now!

The guards immediately forced Mrs Chu onto the floor and proceeded to give her the thirty strokes. The guards let the full force of their battens strike Mrs Chu. She tried to hide her pain, but found that the beatings this time were more severe then the first. She looked at the Judge angrily and screamed louder with each beating.

Judge Quan stared at the accused woman and decided on an even more drastic course of action to break her resolve. He knew that she was strong and that harsher torture was necessary to confuse her and break her.

"I will not hesitate to order more severe torture unless you speak up. Is it not true that you and Candidate Soong plotted to murder me, the Judge of this town? Did you not plan to overthrow this Tribunal? Speak up?"

"No!" Mrs Chu screamed as the beatings continued.

"Did you not plan and scheme in the hope that Candidate Soong himself would become Judge after I was dead or deposed? We all know that Candidate Soong had wide connections. Is that the truth?" Judge Quan shouted back, growing increasingly angry.

"No, I..." Mrs Chu became weaker with each beating as the flesh around her buttocks grew red with blood and each blow of the batten cut through her tender skin. Angry and wary, Mrs Chu began to lose her resolve.

"You thought that if Candidate Soong became Judge Soong you would become famous and respected. You will die. You will die mercilessly for your despicable crimes."

Judge Quan stood up, striking his hands together with each new question. "How dare you treat the people of this town with such mockery? How dare you turn against your Court? How dare you treat Heaven's rule with no respect?" Judge Quan pointed his large fore-finger at Mrs Chu.

"No...we killed Fan-shing so Soong and I could..." Mrs Chu screamed at the Judge and collapsed, oblivious that she had fallen into the Judge's trap. The courtroom buzzed as the people realised that Mrs Chu had admitted killing her husband.

While the guards were bringing some sour tea for the woman, Judge Quan ordered that Candidate Soong be brought to the court. By this time, Mrs Chu was fully aware of her surroundings. She saw her paramour kneel face down in front of the Judge and she was afraid even to glance at him. Her defiance and resolve had been broken, partly by the pain from the beatings and partly because she was now aware that she had let the truth slip out.

"Mrs Chu, you have just said that you killed Fan-shing. This man, Candidate Soong, has accused you of planning to kill your husband, the Rice-merchant and Examiner Shao. Do not put yourself through more pain, Mrs Chu. Tell the court the complete truth."

"Did you? Did you say that about me?" Mrs Chu asked Candidate Soong?

Still afraid to look at Mrs Chu, the Candidate nodded his head in agreement to her question.

Mrs Chu looked up and around the courtroom. The people she had relied on and whom previously she had always persuaded to be on her side all looked away.

"The Court heard, while Mrs Chu was in her deepest agony, a partial confession of her crime," Judge Quan said. "This Court will not hesitate to obtain her full confession so that justice may be fully served. Guards, give her another thirty lashes." The Judge departed from his own resolve to treat Mrs Chu with dignity.

As the guards let the full force of their battens strike the now torn skin of Mrs Chu, she let out a loud cry of agony with each beating. Judge Quan and the people in court wondered how much pain Mrs Chu could take before she confessed. Suddenly her body fell, limp and lifeless. The Judge quickly ordered the guards to stop and again provide her with sour tea. When it was apparent that she was too weak to drink, the Judge realized that he had gone too far. Though she was young, her body apparently could not endure two consecutive punishments. He ordered that she be taken back to her prison cell for later questioning. He also suggested that the Coroner should assist her. So far, thought the Judge, Mrs Chu had been stubborn and full of pride.

Persuading an accused to confess through torture was one thing, but causing death through torture would have dire consequences for him. He knew of many past cases when the presiding Judge had been prosecuted for his negligence. In the circumstances, the Judge thought that justice would have to wait.

He rapped the gavel and said that the Tribunal would continue questioning Mrs Chu at the afternoon session. He then announced that the morning session was closed.

Back at the Tribunal library, Judge Quan slumped back on his seat in frustration, as he had been unable to break Mrs Chu's resolve. Already the case had taken a great deal of time and the Judge could not help but wonder how a more experienced Magistrate would have quickly resolved and wrapped up a similar case in fewer days.

E-Lung looked at the Judge, aware that he was lost in thought. For many days he had observed the low and the high points of the case and the Judge's composure and perseverance had impressed him.

The silence was broken only when Coroner Chen entered the library and announced that Mrs Chu had regained consciousness but was still very weak. He felt that she would not be able to stand further punishment as this might cause her permanent injury, or kill her.

"What was the state of her mind when she came to?" asked the Judge, interested in whether her resolve had finally been broken.

"Slightly distraught but that is only to be expected after what she has gone through. When she saw me, she quickly moved away and refused any treatment. I had to instruct a cell guard to assist her."

The Judge sat back on his chair and for a while there was silence in the room. He looked at his two loyal assistants. Although he appreciated their loyalty, he felt he needed some time alone to consider his next move against Mrs Chu.

"Did you two not say you would celebrate upon the successful completion of the murder case? We have already pieced together the puzzle. All we need is to obtain the confession of the culprit."

The two men now realized that their Magistrate needed time alone. They excused themselves from the Judge's presence and left the library. E-Lung looked at the Coroner and said jokingly, as they left the Tribunal, "You've been in this town longer then I have. Introduce me to some special local cuisine and don't disappoint me. I have an abiding interest in food!"

Judge Quan sat alone in the library, trying to distract his thoughts by routine work. But he was unable to put Mrs Chu out of his mind. So he then sat looking intently at Fan-shing's painting. Judge Quan thought he had given Mrs Chu enough opportunities to confess. Yet she was still defiant. He had had enough. Tomorrow, he would bring Fan-shing back from the dead and let him confront Mrs Chu.

CHAPTER TWENTY-ONE

*During those lonely nights, crying and sleeping by myself,
many thoughts passed through my mind.*

A cold green mist encircled the prison cell and Mrs Chu. Slowly, it dissipated and she found herself standing in the middle of an old suspension bridge. She could hear the loud cracks of wooden planks as the old bridge swayed back and forth in the wind.

From a distance she saw Fan-shing with his arms stretched out, inviting her to come to him. She took a step forward and suddenly Fan-shing's face turned dark revealing large blue bruises, symptoms of white cloud poison. She stepped back in fright as Fan-shing began to laugh. Turning to run back, she saw Judge Quan clad in his imposing Magistrate's clothes. His hands were crossed and he was looking at her angrily. She turned round to run towards her husband, but saw him cutting the rope to the bridge with a long silver knife. Suddenly, the bridge dropped a fraction as Fan-shing's laughter grew louder. The bridge began to turn sideways and, unable to maintain her grip, Mrs Chu fell headlong into a dark abyss. She screamed to her husband for help, but could only see him and Judge Quan laughing as she fell. Her hair grew whiter and her face became wrinkled with old age until finally her face was nothing but that of a skeleton, crying aloud for mercy.

Mrs Chu awoke in the midst of her cry as she heard the gates of the prison cell open. Two guards entered, slowly eased her off her bed and then brought her to court. She looked frantically around for her husband, cold sweat flowing freely down her back. She was frightened and deluded by the nightmare she had experienced.

Judge Quan sat still in his court after giving orders for the Warden and Candidate Soong to be brought out. As all three of the accused knelt in front of the Judge, the people in the packed courtroom gazed at the trio, all three of whom were accused of committing desperate and cruel crimes.

"This court has in the past few days uncovered a crime that involved the murder of three innocent people. Mrs Chu, your lover, Candidate Soong, has admitted his involvement in a plan to plot the murder of your husband, Fan-shing, as well as the murders of the Rice-merchant and Examiner Shao. The Warden here has also admitted to carrying out your plans for the murder of three innocent people. So you see, Mrs Chu, your two accomplices have rid themselves of any emotional guilt through their confessions in court. You will have to live in Fan-shing's shadow for the rest of your life."

Every time the Judge mentioned her husband, shivers passed through Mrs Chu's body. She looked down, silent and dejected. The nightmare involving her dead and revengeful husband, as well as the unforgiving anger of the Judge, had scared the very foundations of her resolve. Even after her husband Fan-shing's death, it seemed, there was no escape from him. She would always be haunted by his ghost. She could not live with him while he was alive. Now, how was she to continue in the presence of his ghostly shadow?

Judge Quan looked at Mrs Chu. Tears flowed freely from her eyes as she cried silently. The previously manipulative, beautiful and elegant Mrs Chu had now been replaced by a frightened and dejected person.

"Look up, Mrs Chu! Even in death your husband Fan-shing speaks to us in his last painting."

The painting was now carried into the courtroom, visible for all to see. Judge Quan stepped down from the dais and stood next to the painting. He then proceeded to explain how Fan-shing knew that his wife was plotting against him by writing down her name, HONG, on the painting in the depiction of a river, trees and horses.

The courtroom was immediately delighted. The people were astounded at Fan-Shing's ingenuity and Judge Quan's deductive capacity.

"It was a clever way for Fan-shing to disguise the murderer's name. He worked night and day on this, his last painting. Usually he spent most of his time drinking heavily and gambling. You told me that yourself, Mrs Chu. But you knew that there was something significant about this painting and you tried to prevent the court from withholding it as evidence. Isn't that right?"

Mrs Chu looked at the painting and then quickly looked away. The Warden and her lover, Candidate Soong, had accused her in court, the two people she had placed so much trust in for so long. When she looked up and saw the Judge standing next to the painting, she instantly took fright. For a moment, she thought she had seen Fan-shing's face in the painting, rather than the gaze of an angry Judge. It was too much.

"Get ...get that painting away from me. I'll answer, but take it away," Mrs Chu begged.

Judge Quan ordered it to be moved aside.

Slowly, after some tea had been given to her, she calmed down and collected herself. She knelt in front of the Judge and began to talk coherently.

"For many years, I saw my mother work day and night sewing clothes to make ends meet. We were terribly poor and I cannot say that my mother was happy, living in the shadow of my father. But luckily I was taken in by a dancing teacher and was given tuition in the arts. For the first time I realized that I had the intelligence and the means to break out of my family's poverty. I swore that I would never be like my mother, subservient to her husband.

"When my family arranged my marriage to Fan-shing, I was only too happy to comply. I wanted to leave home and get away from seeing my mother suffer. But more importantly, Fan-shing was an up-and-coming artist, soon to be rich. Well, at least that's what I was led to believe.

"As months turned into years, I realized that that was only a dream. Fan-shing's paintings were not selling. Increasingly he stayed out most of the time, drinking and gambling, and soon we were broke. I tried to do my best by conducting dance classes, but Fan-shing would always beat me and take what little money I earned. With money in his pocket, he would go out again and gamble it all away. Often I was left alone, in tears.

"During those lonely nights, crying and sleeping by myself, many thoughts passed through my mind. I was no better off than when I was living with my mother and my father. I feared that if nothing was done, I would forever be locked in the situation I had witnessed and hated in my younger years. As each night passed and with each new beating I received at the hands of my husband, I became more and more desperate for change.

"When I met Candidate Soong, I knew that he was the man to help me out of my situation. He was rich, reputable and willing. With him I could get rid of Fan-shing and live a good and comfortable life. He, in turn, knew that with me he could enhance his reputation and rid himself from the shadow of his father. It was a match made in Heaven.

"I thought of a plan to kill my husband during those long and lonely nights but I kept those thoughts to myself. I only made my plans known when Fan-shing found out about the Candidate and myself, threatening to tell the court about us and the Candidate's examination result. It was our only hope for Candidate Soong and me to remain together and he agreed with me.

"The plan was to get rid of Fan Shing during his sleep. The Warden was to apply the poison while Candidate Soong would bribe your predecessor to overlook the case favourably. It was a perfect plan until Your Honour's abrupt arrival in town. By then it was too late, I hated my husband, I hated his brutality and I hated our poverty. So I continued with the plan."

Mrs Chu looked at the Judge, this time half laughing and sobbing. Now that her resolve was broken, there was nothing to hold her back from telling the full story. It was a story so brutal and painful that she felt it had to be told truthfully. After all, she knew that she would be executed for her crime. There was nothing to lose. She giggled at the irony that she would soon join her husband in the afterworld, whereas in fact she had wanted to rid herself of him. Her giggle soon turned into hysterical laughter.

"Soon I'll join Fan Shing again. Do you think he will love me? Do you think he will forgive me?" Mrs Chu asked the Judge.

Judge Quan returned to the dais without even a glance at Mrs Chu. He looked around the silent and passive courtroom, aware that not only had three innocent individuals been mercilessly murdered, but also that for the past three days the townspeople had lived in grave fear that a murderer was amongst them. He then looked at Mrs Chu and spoke clearly to the courtroom.

"Today, this Court has revealed the complete truth about the Fan-shing murder case. We have heard how Mrs Chu formulated a plan to murder her husband. It was the Warden who carried out the act while Candidate Soong, Mrs Chu's paramour, acted as an accessory to the murder."

With those words, the Judge immediately closed the afternoon session. As people filed out of the courtroom, they expressed their thanks that Heaven had blessed them with a young but just Magistrate. Life and business in their town could now get back to normality.

As Judge Quan disappeared behind his curtain, an old man with long white hair and beard left his seat in the court. Unbeknown to everyone else around him, the hermit smiled contentedly, satisfied that this Judge had indeed learned his lessons well.

CHAPTER TWENTY-TWO

In this world, hatred can never be appeased by hatred.
Hatred can only be appeased by love. This is the eternal law.
— Dhammapada

The first light of the morning sun shone its rays over a thick mist which hung heavily over the hills beyond the bridge. The thickness and stillness of the mist meant that the hills beyond were not visible to a lonesome Judge Quan as he dismounted from his horse and stood next to the old suspension bridge.

The Judge peered at the bridge's fragile wooden and rope structure but did not dare to cross it. He was deep in thought about the events of the past few days. His face looked strained as he leaned against an old wooden pole which acted as one of the supports for the bridge.

He would become a celebrated man, Judge Quan thought. With the conclusion of the Fan-shing murder case, Judge Quan had sensed a change in the town's attitude towards him. When he travelled in his palanquin to and from the Tribunal, people by the roadside went out of their way to bow to their Magistrate. It was a sign of respect that the Judge had not seen since his arrival in the town.

Coroner Chen and E-Lung had both offered to work permanently with the Tribunal and Judge Quan was happy to accept. He had initially feared that the difficulties of the past few days might have deterred his two assistants. But, somewhat to the Judge's surprise, they expressed their gratitude for his consideration towards them. The difficulties that they had faced were more of a challenge than an obstacle.

Judge Quan felt that he would be better able to perform his tasks efficiently, with the help of his two assistants. He believed that there was still a gap between Coroner Chen and himself, but that time would narrow it. He knew that he would gain from the Coroner's intimate local knowledge and his many years of life experience both as a citizen of the town and as a man of medicine. E-Lung's exceptional skills in the martial arts and his intimate knowledge of military procedures meant that he could be used for more dangerous tasks. Indeed, Judge Quan sensed that the Tribunal officers were now more disciplined and alert since E-Lung had become their commander.

Judge Quan shifted against the bridge supports, sensing that if he wasn't careful, the old wooden structure would give way and he would plunge into the deep ravine as he had in his dream. He stepped back and sat down on a slab of rock, moving his body into a more comfortable posture.

He peered into the mist and tried to make out what lay beyond. He sensed a compulsion to walk across the bridge and meet the old hermit once more, but he felt it would be inappropriate to burden the reclusive hermit with his earthly material thoughts.

It had been a macabre atmosphere during yesterday's afternoon court session. Upon receipt of an official message from the Prefect, Judge Quan convened an afternoon session out in the open in the farming sector, where executions were normally performed, rather than in the tribunal compound. It was attended by almost everyone in town who had seen the specially armoured messenger gallop majestically through the town.

The afternoon court session was convened against the backdrop of a plantation of lush green trees, which swayed gently in the cool afternoon breeze. The Easterly wind had brought a respite from the usually hot and sultry weather, but along with the cool air it had also brought with it frighteningly dark and thick clouds that had already totally enveloped the town.

Judge Quan recalled clearly the words of the verdict brought down by the Provincial Prefect. They were short and sharp. Deliberately composed in a formal manner, they offered little or no compassion for the perpetrators of three hideous crimes.

"In the name of our Illustrious Emperor Tai Zong, Father of our great Empire, ever wise and ever grand, Whose rule has been approved by the Heavens and will be so for many years to come.

"In the case of the late Chu Fan-shing, presided over by Judge Quan Wu-meng, the following verdict has been reached in accordance with the law brought down by the Great Emperor. The man, so-called The Beggar, is found guilty of being an accomplice to the murder of Rice-merchant He. He will be punished to bear the cangue around his neck for three cycles of the moon.

"To the person named Warden of the North-Eastern sector of Sui-chou, who confessed to committing three murders, namely that of Chu Fan-shing, Rice-merchant He and Examiner Shao, May a Thousand Swords commit him to death.

"To the person named Candidate Soong, one and only son of the eminent Soong Fu-liu. For his crime of an adulterous affair and a conspiracy to murder the afore-mentioned three men, May a Thousand Swords commit him to death. However, due to his father's services to this Empire, the sentence of death by a Thousand Swords is commuted to death by Strangulation.

"To the person named Chu Hong-li, who confessed to plotting a murder against her husband Chu Fan-shing and in the process was also involved in a plot to murder Merchant He and Examiner Shao, may a Thousand Swords also commit her to death.

"Let it be known such extreme crimes are not tolerated by the Empire and within the confines of human souls and dignity. There is only one justice and that is through the courts. Let this be a lesson to all, that such acts will be dealt with promptly and severely with the ultimate punishments the law is able to meet out."

Judge Quan shifted uneasily, partly to find a more comfortable position, while at the same time recollecting events during the execution. It was his first time as Judge to preside over the more macabre proceedings of the court. He had wanted to forget these events, but he also realized that they had gravely disturbed him. He thought that he had better confront them once more, before they affected his life. Closing his eyes, he cast his mind back to the sentences that had been imposed.

The beggar received the lightest sentence of the four perpetrators, being punished to wear the cangue for the next three cycles of the moon. The cangue is a large heavy wooden board consisting of two joined pieces, each cut on the inside in the shape of a semi-circle. The two pieces are closed around the neck of a prisoner and locked. For as long as he wears it, he cannot reach his mouth to feed himself. At the same time, the prisoner's hands and legs are chained together, restricting mobility. For the next three cycles of the moon then, the circumstances in which the beggar would seek his food would be much worse than usual. He would suffer the humiliation of begging from passers-by; some – less sympathetic – would spit at him or throw dirt at him. He would have to endure the hot sun, and his only respite would be the darkness of night.

A cowardly man, who struggled vainly against the court officers and begged aloud to be free, had now replaced the previously aggravated and aggressive Candidate Soong. He was placed faced down on the ground with both his hands and legs tied. A large executioner sat astride on top of the Candidate's back, which effectively pinned him down. He then placed a noose around the Candidate's neck and looked at the Judge. Once Judge Quan gave the signal to proceed, the noose was quickly tightened and the Candidate's body lifted above the ground as he convulsed violently. The crowd was silent. Only the wind could be heard. Slowly, the Candidate's face turned blue and his body gradually became limp and lifeless.

It was an appropriate sentence, the Judge thought. Although in this life the Candidate had erred, he could at least present his body intact in the world beyond. In doing so, it gave him the opportunity to be reborn as a better person. This was the Candidate's second chance for a better life, not in this life, but a subsequent life.

The Warden and Mrs Chu were tied separately to wooden crosses. As they were brought forth, they both saw the limp body of Candidate Soong. The Warden was calm, probably resigned to the fact that nothing could now save him. On the other hand, Mrs Chu was laughing and crying hysterically. Judge Quan was overwhelmed by her screams. These reminded him of his dream, so much so that he couldn't bear the sight of what was to come, ordering that both should be executed simultaneously. He further ordered that Mrs Chu should be killed by the fourth cut of the sword and the Warden by the second. After that, their bodies would be further cut by the executioners beyond recognition and the heads severed and displayed at the market square for all to see.

A second executioner stood next to the first. Both men carried long, curved and glistening swords. They both looked at the Judge, waiting for the signal to proceed.

The signal was given and the first cut sliced the Warden's chest, while the second skillfully struck the same area on Mrs Chu. Blood splashed forth instantly to the horror of the crowd and the cries of agony from both man and woman were drowned by the ever-increasing sounds of the wind. The first executioner waited while the second sliced Mrs Chu's face. Instantly her nose fell to the ground. The first executioner then stabbed the Warden's heart until his sword protruded from the rear of his body. The Warden's blood flowed freely from the front and rear of the sword. It was a mortal cut and the Warden's screams of agony fell silent. Just as quickly, the second executioner sliced Mrs Chu's throat and her blood once more splashed out as her screams fell silent. Her body continued to sway silently from side to side. Another strong jab to her heart was the final mortal cut and her body suddenly became still. Despite the fact that the convicts were already dead, both executioners continued to cut into both bodies until the hands and legs were severed. Finally, after a considerable time, they severed the heads which fell silently onto the ground.

Although death by strangulation was a more painful form of death, it left the body intact and was a means for the spirit of that person to be reborn. Death by a Thousand Swords on the other hand comes quickly on the second or fourth cut, but the spirit cannot recognise itself in the world beyond, since the head has been decapitated. The person's violent acts in this life make him or her unworthy to be reborn.

Judge Quan shivered when he recalled the final cuts of the swords and the heads rolling off from the bodies. Cold sweat ran freely down his forehead as he clumsily wiped it with his long sleeves. He shook his head and gave a deep sigh as he reflected on the dire consequences of one's actions.

The Warden's acceptance of Candidate Soong's help to raise him from the streets may have been the worst decision of his life. Although it was natural to accept such a kind offer, if he had not accepted Candidate Soong's help, he could still be alive and able to determine his own destiny, rather than having other people dictate what he should do against his own will.

On the other hand, Candidate Soong had had wealth and reputation, but had suffered from the rigid upbringing of a stern father. The Candidate had found himself trapped in a life that required him to live up to other people's expectations, and he was constantly measured in comparison with his father. However, if he had been true to his studies, he would not have let a person such as Mrs Chu stand in his way. She used him as a tool for her own benefit and ultimately he had to pay for the lack of discipline in his life.

For Mrs Chu, the Judge had little pity. Although she had suffered from an abusive husband, there were other means she could have found to deal with her problem rather than take the extreme action of killing him. It was true that she had been abused; but Judge Quan could not overlook the fact that she had wanted to be famous and had believed that, with her husband the artist Fan-shing, she could never realize those dreams.

Judge Quan felt a sense of sorrow as he knew that for as long as there was hatred against others, greed for material gain and minds clouded by corruption, there would always be violent and hideous crimes. He was an official, a man who had sworn to his deceased parents that justice would be served to the people. No, the Judge thought, he must be strong and determined and free himself from such unwholesome thoughts and actions.

He stood up and told himself that he would never let fear impede his lifelong tasks as Magistrate. In order to prove his determination, he strode forth and slowly walked across the bridge without hesitation. The old and squeaking bridge swayed up and down as the Magistrate made his way to the hills beyond.

He reappeared from the thick mist on the other side of the bridge. On this side, the sun shone brightly. He felt the warmth of the rays soothing and easing his tense body and he felt that his inner spirit and strength had been rejuvenated. He turned around and saw the mist gradually form into a figure, this time a male.

It was the majestic old hermit who now stood in front of him, both hands reaching out to the Judge as he spoke. "Judge Quan Wu-meng, you have learned well. You have realized that fear can be harnessed and used for the benefit of others, If you always maintain this thought, you will, in effect, overcome fear."

Judge Quan awoke suddenly at his library desk. He rubbed his eyes with both hands and settled back in his chair. His fears were at rest. He was at peace with himself. ~ ~

AUTHOR'S ACKNOWLEDGEMENTS

I would like to express my appreciation to some people who are very important to me: my parents for their sacrifice in migrating to Australia to provide a better life for their children; my wife Susan Chan, whom I met more than twelve years ago, while writing this novel. Now we are happily married and have a young son, Ethan, whose constant questions are a delight!

I also thank the Founders, Judges and Administrators of the Proverse Prize for Unpublished Non-fiction, Fiction and Poetry for recommending that my 2010 entry should be published. Finally, Revenge From Beyond is available for readers to see. Last but not least, I am most grateful for the hard work, long hours and patience of my Proverse Editors. If I were not the author, I might even say, the final manuscript is a delight to read.

REFERENCES

J. Dyer Ball, *The Chinese at home.* The Religious Tract Society. 1st ed.

Frena Bloomfield, *The book of Chinese beliefs.* 1st Ed. Great Britain, Arrow Books Ltd., 1983 (reprints 1985, 1986).

Herbert A. Gilles, His yuan lu "Instructions to coroners". Royal Society of Medicine. 1st ed. 1874 (republished 1924).

Robert Van Gulik, *Tang yin pi shih "parallel cases from under the pear tree".* Hyperion Press. 1992 (reprint of 1956 Edition).

T. C. Lai, *A Scholar in Imperial China.* 1st ed. Hong Kong, Kelly and Walsh Ltd., 1970.

John Merson, *Roads to Xanadu; East and West in the Making of the Modern World,* 1st ed, ABC/ Child Australia, Wiedenfeld & Nicholson UK (1989).

Ichisada Miyazaki, *China's examination hell – the civil service examinations of Imperial China.* 1st ed. New York, Weatherhill, 1976.

Life behind the great wall. Hong Kong, Reader's Digest Association, 1st. ed. 1996.

Martin Palmer, *Tung Shu – The Chinese almanac.* 1st Ed. USA, Shambhala Publications Inc., 1986.

PROVERSE HONG KONG

Proverse Hong Kong is based in Hong Kong with long-term and expanding regional and international connections.

Proverse has published novels, novellas, fictionalized autobiography, non-fiction (including autobiography, biography, history, memoirs, sport, travel narratives), single-author poetry collections, children's, teens / young adult and academic books. Other interests include diaries, and academic works in the humanities, social sciences, cultural studies, linguistics and education. Some Proverse books have accompanying audio texts. Some are translated into Chinese.

Proverse welcomes authors who have a story to tell, wisdom, perceptions or information to convey, a person they want to memorialize, a neglect they want to remedy, a record they want to correct, a strong interest that they want to share, skills they want to teach, and who consciously seek to make a contribution to society in an informative, interesting and well-written way. Proverse works with texts by non-native-speaker writers of English as well as by native English-speaking writers.

The name, "Proverse", combines the words "prose" and "verse" and is pronounced accordingly.

THE PROVERSE PRIZE

The Proverse Prize, an annual international competition for an unpublished book-length work of fiction, non-fiction, or poetry, was established in January 2008. It is open to all who are at least eighteen on the date they sign the entry form. Unusually for a competition of this nature, there is no restriction based on nationality, residence or citizenship.

The objectives of the Proverse Prize are: to encourage excellence and / or excellence and usefulness in publishable written work in the English Language, which can, in varying degrees, "delight and instruct". Entries are invited from anywhere in the world. Semi-finalists to date include writers born or resident in Andorra, Australia, Canada, Germany, Hong Kong, New Zealand, Nigeria, Singapore, South Africa, Taiwan, The Bahamas, the Peoples' Republic of China, the United Arab Emirates, the United Kingdom, the USA.

Founders: Verner Bickley and Gillian Bickley. To celebrate their lifelong love of words in all their forms as readers, writers, editors, academics, performers, and publishers.
Honorary Legal Advisor: Mr Raymond T. L. Tse.
Honorary Accountant: Mr Neville Chow.
Honorary Judges: Anonymous.
Honorary Advisors: Bahamian poet Marion Bethel; UK translator, Margaret Clarke; UK linguist & lexicographer David Crystal; Canadian poet and academic, Jonathan Hart; Swedish linguist Björn Jernudd; Hong Kong University Librarian, Peter Sidorko; Singapore poet Edwin Thumboo; Czech novelist & poet Olga Walló.
Honorary UK agent and distributor: Christine Penney
Honorary Administrators: Proverse Hong Kong.

Proverse Prize Winners Whose Books Have Already Been Published By Proverse Hong Kong

Laura Solomon, Rebecca Jane Tomasis, Gillian Jones,
David Diskin, Peter Gregoire, Sophronia Liu, Birgit Linder,
James McCarthy, Celia Claase, Philip Chatting.

Summary Terms and Conditions
(for indication only & subject to revision)

The information below is for guidance only. Please refer to the year-specific Proverse Prize Entry Form & Terms & Conditions, which are uploaded in April each year onto the Proverse Hong Kong website: <www.proversepublishing.com>.

The free Proverse E-Newsletter includes ongoing information about the Proverse Prize. To be put on the E-Newsletter mailing-list, email: info@proversepublishing.com with your request.

Revenge from Beyond

The Prize
1) Publication by Proverse Hong Kong, with
2) Cash prize of HKD10,000 (HKD7.80 = approx. US$1.00)

Supplementary publication grants may be made to selected other entrants for publication by Proverse Hong Kong.

Depending on the quality of the work in any year, the prize may be shared by at most two entrants or withheld, as recommended by the judges.

In 2015, the entry fee was: HKD220.00 OR GBP32.00.

Writers are eligible, who are at least eighteen on the date they sign The Proverse Prize entry documents. There is no nationality or residence restriction.

Each submitted work must be an unpublished publishable single-author work of non-fiction, fiction or poetry, the original work of the entrant, and submitted in the English language. School textbooks and plays are ineligible.

Translated work: If the work entered is a translation from a language other than English, both the original work and the translation should be previously unpublished. The submitted work will not be judged as a translation but as an original work.

Extent of the Manuscript: within the range of what is usual for the genre of the work submitted. However, it is advisable that novellas be in the range 30,000 to 45,000 words); other fiction (e.g. novels, short-story collections) and non-fiction (e.g. autobiographies, biographies, diaries, letters, memoirs, essay collections, etc.) should be in the range, 75,000 to 100,000 words. Poetry collections should be in the range, 5,000 to 25,000 words. Other word-counts and mixed-genre submissions are not ruled out.

Writers may choose, if they wish, to obtain the services of an Editor in presenting their work, and should acknowledge this help and the nature and extent of this help in the Entry Form.

**KEY DATES FOR THE PROVERSE PRIZE
IN ANY YEAR
(subject to confirmation and/or change)**

Receipt of Entry Fees / Entry Documents	[No later than] 14 April to 31 May
Receipt of entered manuscripts	1 May to 30 June
Announcement of semi-finalists	July-September
Announcement of finalists	October-December
Announcement of winner/ max two winners (sharing the cash prize)	December of the year of entry to April of the year that follows the year of entry
Cash Award made	At the same time as publication of the work(s) adjudged the winner / joint-winners of the Proverse Prize
Publication of winning work(s)	In or after November of the year that follows the year of entry

Revenge from Beyond

NOVELS, SHORT STORY COLLECTIONS
AND OTHER FICTION
Published by Proverse Hong Kong

If you have enjoyed *Revenge from Beyond* by Dennis Wong,
you may also enjoy Caleb Kavon's *The Reluctant Terrorist.*

You may also like to read the following
(all titles in English unless otherwise stated)

A Misted Mirror, by Gillian Jones. 2011.
A Painted Moment, by Jennifer Ching. 2010.
An Imitation of Life, by Laura Solomon. 2013.
Article 109, by Peter Gregoire. 2012.
Bao Bao's Odyssey: from Mao's Shanghai to Capitalist Hong Kong, by Paul Ting. 2012.
Black Tortoise Winter, by Jan Pearson. Scheduled 2015 / 2016.
Bright Lights and White Nights, by Andrew Carter. 2015.
cemetery miss you, by Jason S Polley. 2011.
Cop Show Heaven, by Lawrence Gray. 2015.
Death has a Thousand Doors, by Patricia Grey. 2011.
Hilary and David, by Laura Solomon. 2011.
Instant Messages, by Laura Solomon. 2010.
Man's Last Song, by James Tam. 2013.
Mila the Magician, by Zhang Jian. 2013. (English / Chinese bilingual)
Mishpacha – Family, by Rebecca Tomasis. 2010.
Odds and Sods, by Lawrence Gray. 2013.
Paranoia (the Walk and Talk with Angela), by Caleb Kavon. 2012.
Red Bird Summer, by Jan Pearson. 2014.
Revenge from Beyond, by Dennis Wong. 2011.
The Day They Came, by Gérard Louis Breissan. 2012.
The Devil You know, by Peter Gregoire. 2014.
The Monkey in Me: Confusion, Love and Hope under a Chinese Sky, by Caleb Kavon. 2009.
The Monkey in Me, by Caleb Kavon. Translated by Chapman Chen. 2010. E-book. 2010. (Chinese)
The Perilous Passage of Princess Petunia Peasant, by Victor Edward Apps. 2014.

The Reluctant Terrorist: in Search of the Jizo, by Caleb Kavon. 2011.
The Shingle Bar Sea Monster and Other Stories, by Laura Solomon. 2012.
The Snow Bridge and Other Stories, by Philip Chatting. Scheduled 2015.
Tiger Autumn, by Jan Pearson. 2015.
The Village in the Mountains, by David Diskin. 2012.
Tightrope! A Bohemian Tale, by Olga Walló. Translated from Czech by Johanna Pokorny, Veronika Revická & others. 2010.
Tightrope! A Bohemian Tale, by Olga Walló. Translated by Chapman Chen. 2011. (Chinese)
University Days, by Laura Solomon. 2014.
Vera Magpie, by Laura Solomon. 2013.

OTHER GENRES

We also publish in other genres, including autobiography, biography, children's illustrated books, educational books, Hong Kong educational and legal history, memoirs, poetry, teenage / young adult books, and travel. Other genres may be added.

WRITE TO US!

We are interested to read your response to
Dennis Wong's *Revenge from Beyond*
and any other of our publications.
Please write to our email address, proverse@netvigator.com,
giving us a few sentences which you are willing for us to publish,
giving your comments on this book.
If what you write is chosen to be included
in our E-Newsletter or website,
we will select another title published by Proverse
and send you a complimentary copy.
Please include your name, email address and mailing address
when you write to us, and state whether or not we may cut or
edit your comments for publication.
We will use your initials to attribute your comments.

Revenge from Beyond

FIND OUT MORE ABOUT OUR AUTHORS
AND BOOKS

Visit our website
http://www.proversepublishing.com

Visit our distributor's website
<www.chineseupress.com>

Follow us on Twitter
Follow news and conversation: <twitter.com/Proversebooks>
OR
Copy and paste the following to your browser window and
follow the instructions: https://twitter.com/#!/ProverseBooks

'Like us' on Facebook: www.facebook.com/ProversePress

Request our E-Newsletter
Send your request to info@proversepublishing.com.

Availability
Most titles are available in Hong Kong and world-wide
from our Hong Kong based Distributor,
The Chinese University Press of Hong Kong,
The Chinese University of Hong Kong, Shatin, NT,
Hong Kong SAR, China. Email: cup-bus@cuhk.edu.hk

All titles are available from Proverse Hong Kong
and the Proverse Hong Kong UK-based Distributor.

We have stock-holding retailers in Hong Kong,
Singapore (Select Books), Canada (Elizabeth Campbell Books),
Principality of Andorra (Llibreria La Puça, La Llibreria).

Orders can be made from bookshops in the UK and elsewhere.

Ebooks
Most of our titles are available also as Ebooks.